THE DOG RUNNER

BREN MACDIBBLE

Old Barn Books

MIX
Paper from
responsible sources
FSC® C104608
FSC
www.fsc.org

AN OLD BARN BOOK
First published in Australia by Allen & Unwin 2019
This UK edition first published by Old Barn Books in 2019
Copyright © Bren MacDibble 2019

Old Barn Books Ltd
Warren Barn
West Sussex
RH20 1JW

Email: info@oldbarnbooks.com
Web: www.oldbarnbooks.com
Follow us on facebook, twitter or instagram: @oldbarnbooks
Teaching resources for our books are available to download from
our website

ISBN: 9781910646489
Cover and text design by Jo Hunt

Printed in Denmark

First UK edition
10 9 8 7 6 5 4 3 2 1

To all the kids who are not brave
but do brave things anyway.

BE WITH ME
WHEN I WAKE UP

Even with my ear pressed to the floor so hard it hurts, I can't hardly see under Alvie's door.

'Mr Alvie Moore?' I say. 'You still there?'

'Just getting your book, Ella!' he calls, voice all old-raspy.

'Why can't you open the door no more?' I ask.

'Nailed it shut with boards. Ain't no one coming through that door ever again, the way I nailed it shut.'

'But, Mr Alvie Moore, what if there's a fire?' I ask his shuffling slippers through the under-door crack, then sit up to rub my sore ear.

'I'll be barbecue. Don't you worry, I'll open the door

1

when the army arrives to sort out these streets.' Alvie tries to shove a book through the crack but it's too thick and conks against the door. He picks it up, grunts, and then half a paperback, torn right down the spine, slides under the door. I have to wait for the other half to figure out what book he's lending me. Then the top half with the cover comes sliding under the door. It's got a splash of black and a splash of red on the cover that looks like blood. 'Lord of the Flies' in scary black writing.

'You read that one, Ella?' Alvie asks.

'No,' I say, picking up the two halves and putting them back together.

'Good, let me know what you think of it,' Alvie says.

'Thank you! See you when the army gets here,' I say and head back down the stairs, jumping two feet at once, step to step, twenty-two steps to our landing. Emery's too-big hand-me-down shorts need holding for every bounce. Dad gave me these old Emery clothes when he bagged up and threw out all my clothes, saying I was too big for them, even though some of them fit fine. Now I've only got Emery's old clothes.

There are only three floors in this old building. We've got Alvie Moore above, Nontha Mantu below, and us in the middle. Me, Dad, Emery and three dogs, but we're

2

not supposed to say about the dogs. And Mum when she comes home. Nontha's good. She never complains about the clacking of the dogs' toenails on the floor above her head.

I open the door and push through the bouncing fur and licking tongues, rubbing each furry head hello, and smooching my cheek into three big fluffy yowling doggo heads, then I tell Dad what Alvie Moore's gone and done to his door.

He laughs and goes back to trying to stick some wires into an old hand crank from what used to be part of an electric bike, but there are so many bits on the kitchen table, I don't think it's gonna ever spit out any electricity. 'The army? He's waiting for the army? Someone needs to tell that old man an army marches on its stomach, so Australia's got no army!' he says.

'Don't we gotta go and get him out?' I ask. 'What if there's a fire?'

'I'm not sure nailing the door shut isn't a bad idea. The world's turned upside down, Baby Bell, if we wanna survive, we've all got to figure out...'

'How to walk on our heads!' I shout, finishing it for him coz he's said it so many times.

Dad rubs my hair, still stiff and spiky-short from

where he cut it with his shaver last week, so I look like a pale version of Emery.

'What book did you get?' He picks the two pieces out of my hands and turns them over. 'Oh,' he says, his smile sliding away.

'What?' I ask, with him already moving to put the pieces on the top shelf of the bookcase where he thinks I can't reach.

'It's not appropriate,' he says.

'I've read the appropriate ones,' I say. 'There's nothing in the building left for me to read!'

'Yeah, but not that. It's too scary for you.'

'But Dad!' I say. 'I'm not a baby. If it gets too scary, I'll stop reading!'

'Sweetie, there's enough society breaking down outside our door without reading about it for fun.'

'Can I read it then?' Emery calls from his bedroom.

Dad rolls his eyes at me and doesn't answer. Sometimes Emery says stuff just to make people argue with him. But not me. He never argues with me, coz I'm the little sister and he's the big brother, and he looks out for me, no matter what.

'Can I?' Emery yells again.

Dad puts his finger to his lips, ducks down and hides

behind the couch. He's skinny and small, our dad, so he can fold himself down real good.

Maroochy, our biggest black dog, follows him, and Wolf tries to too, but there's not much room down there. A fluffy wagging brown tail is sticking out. Dad waves a hand for me to hide, so I duck behind the armchair, and when Bear comes licking at my face, I wrap myself around him to scrunch him in there too.

There's a huffing and bare feet slapping on the floor tiles as Emery comes out to see why we're not answering. He comes all the way into the lounge room.

'I can see you!' he says.

Dad leaps out then, yelling, 'Dog pile!' He grabs Emery, pulls him onto the couch, Emery wailing and squirming as Dad and me and two big dogs pile on top, giggling and laughing and whining. I bounce off pretty quick coz I weigh even less than the dogs. I leap back on top again.

Maroochy though, she's trying to save Emery from the pile. She's got his jeans leg and is tugging it out from under the pile.

We roll off and Emery slides off the couch and goes skating across the floor with Maroochy tug, tug, tugging him.

'Roochy!' Emery yells, too busy holding his jeans up to stop the slide.

'She saved you!' I yell. 'Good, Roochy!'

She stops dragging and dances around like she's the best, and she really is. I wrap my arms around her big neck and bury my face in her fur, and Emery does too.

'You're a big goose,' Emery says. Then he grabs me and carries me to the couch and drops me down and plonks down beside me. Dogs scramble up on top of us, Dad plops down beside us.

'We're a goosey family!' Dad says and laughs.

But I don't laugh coz we're not a family without Mum. 'We will be when mother goose gets home,' I say.

'Mother Goose is something from a kid's book,' Emery says.

'I mean our mother goose, Mum, you goose.'

I dig my elbow into Emery's side and he squirms, and mutters, 'Not my mum,' like it's a habit he can't stop. Dad gives him a quick eyebrow tweak to tell him he's annoying.

'Why can't she come home now the power's gone out?' I ask Dad, coz that's her job, to keep the power working, that's why she's away from home. But if there's no power for her to keep going, she can come home.

'I'm sure she's on her way, Baby Bell,' Dad says, and wraps a skinny arm around me. His arms are skinny but all muscle, so his hugs are strong. 'The gates are down across the city. I'm sure there's a way for her to get home now.'

'But how?' I ask, coz the city was divided up into a lot of burbs when the food ran out, and rations had to be delivered to each gate, and the only people allowed to leave where they worked that day were the people who were not 'Essential Personnel'. A whole lot of doctors and nurses and policemen and power employees haven't come home to their families for eight months. And since the power went out three weeks ago, there's not even been phone calls.

'You know your mum,' Dad says. 'She's probably got a solar-powered armoured car smashing down the rubbish in the streets right now.'

I laugh at the idea, and even Emery laughs, coz that's the thing about Mum, she's always designing, dreaming, working. That's how come she got into solar power early when Dad was still learning coal power, and how they met when she took over his job. They tell us the story all the time. I think to warn us to always be looking ahead. Emery thinks the story makes Dad look stupid, but Dad made a nice business from home, fixing old electrical things, and he was around to look after me, and Emery when Emery's mum sent him back to the city to live. Dad's better with kids than Mum. She never could slow down enough to just hang out.

Every morning I wake up and think today's the day Mum will make it home. But every night when I go to sleep, the noises down in the street of people out of control is louder and louder, and I wonder how Mum is gonna get through all that to be with me when I wake up.

ME, EMERY AND THREE BIG DOGGOS

Screams in the night. Far away and lonely. Angry shouts. Slamming doors. Breaking glass. A man runs down the street below us, boots thudding on the road, something shiny in his hand flashes as he passes under our only solar street light.

Me, I freeze to stop from breathing in, coz it wouldn't be just a breath, it'd be a sob that sets me crying, and I have to be calm. It's the same as every night out there. But this time, I've not got Dad or Emery here to look out for me.

Maroochy, beside me, growls, puts her paw on the window and stares down, twisting her head, following the man running on, like she thinks he ain't s'posed to be out there after the curfew sirens have sounded.

'It's okay, Roochy,' I whisper, and bury my hand deep in the warm fur of her neck. Not allowed to cry, Emery said. Maroochy will be worried. You have to look out for Maroochy, he said, like I'm stupid enough to believe that. He left Maroochy here to guard me, that's for sure. I just nodded, couldn't say a thing, and he slipped out the door, leaving me here alone, 'cept for Rooch. Him going out into the city, just like Dad did twelve days ago, just like Mum did eight months ago.

'He'll come back,' I whisper into Maroochy's fuzzy triangle ear. 'They'll all come back.' But it's already gone dark, and that's when Emery said he'd be back.

Curfew's not even a thing now, even with sirens blaring at seven every night, and me wondering every single time how they still got power. The barriers around the suburbs are broken down. No guards are standing there to stop night-time looters no more. Dad said they'd run to save their own necks and we should too, soon as Mum gets here. Emery said Mum could take care of herself. She was probably safe somewhere anyway. Emery said we don't need to wait for her. He said he wasn't going to wait for Jackie one day more. I heard them talking at night when they thought I was sleeping. Emery said he had to get to his grandad, coz his Ba knew about grass and the land and stuff and he needed Emery to help him. Emery said he'd go alone. Dad was angry, but he said he'd go get Mum then we could leave together. Dad said the government was promising us food that they can't get hold of, and the city was just gonna break down when it didn't show up.

Down the street, where the ethanol bus ground to a stop last year and nobody bothered moving it, someone lights a fire in the old ripped-off car bonnet. It's real dark except for that one solar light and the sparking fire. People come out of houses up the street looking this way and that, like they don't trust no one, carrying pots of water to put on the old shopping trolley tipped sideways that we use for a grille in the middle of that car-bonnet fire. Adding old bits of furniture they don't want, to keep the fire going. They don't bring out what food they got now though, nobody trusting nobody no more in case they take it for themselves. Better to eat that can of fish just stood heating in the boiling water than have someone smell it cooking and snatch it away.

Used to be me and Emery down there at the fire too, talking to the neighbours, playing ball with our dogs under street lights when we had them, but then the government stopped delivering food parcels so often, no more cans of fish, no more dried soup bones and vegetables. Dad said we shouldn't let anyone know we got the dogs still, him playing ball with them on the stairs and sneaking them down to pee and poop in the little backyard after checking no one was around to see.

So it was me, Dad, and Emery, and our three big doggos in a tiny upstairs flat day after day coz Dad didn't want us going to school, ever since the suburbs were fenced off from each other, after Mum went out to work and couldn't get back in.

It's been so long since I been to school. Lucky for me, I got my reading going good, coz with no power and nowhere to play, it's just me carrying books upstairs to old Alvie Moore or downstairs to Nontha Mantu to see if they got some books to swap that maybe I can read.

Some days, I wish I could go to school to see my friends and use the swings, but Dad says I always gotta be ready to do as he tells me, coz that's the only way he can keep us all safe.

'Soon as he gets back, I'll do whatever he tells me,' I whisper to Maroochy, coz there's no one but her keeping me safe right now.

I kick at the backpack by my feet, waiting for me to haul on. Most of it's taken up by a beautiful tin of Anzac bickies I been saving, but my boot toe don't hit the tin. I get down on the floor and shove my hand in the backpack, feeling all around past my two changes of clothes and my toothbrush. Only some little cans of sardines. Emery's taken my Anzacs to trade. I dunno what's better to trade for than a big tin of bickies. My face gets real hot that he didn't even ask me or tell me what he'd be trading them for. Him just going off trading for both of us like he's the adult and I'm a baby.

My belly grumbles like it knows already it won't be getting Anzacs ever again.

That ugly red fungus killed all the wheat for flour, killed all the oats, killed the sugar cane for sugar and golden syrup, along with all the grass for cows and butter. Killed just about every ingredient that me and Dad used when we made Anzac bickies. I don't think I'll ever see another Anzac bickie in my whole life.

I find a tube of toothpaste, open it and smear it on my teeth, suck it off. I get another fingerful for Maroochy, who licks it and keeps making licking noises as she tries to deal with stuff that's not really food. Both of us sitting in the dark, sucking at our teeth, worrying.

13

Maroochy's dark eyes flash in the light from the fire down the street as she waves her head around chasing toothpaste on her muzzle. Poor Maroochy. She don't understand why we can't feed her more than a can of sardines a day. She don't know why that rush of raw meat stopped coming. After the grass died from that ugly red fungus, we had a lot of starving sheep and cows that needed eating, and it was fine times for Maroochy all right. She got fat, her black fur shiny and glossy like crow feathers, even as the world changed all around us. But now that's gone, and we're all just living on our own fat and whatever else we've saved to get us through. Me, Emery, and three big doggos.

'We're gonna starve if we stay here,' Emery said. 'If we're gonna go, best go now.' And he said it like going was something easy. Like all we have to do is walk away.

LIPSTICK ON
THE WALLS

Maroochy is malamute and black shepherd. She's our biggest dog, so she's probably the hungriest, and the smartest, even maybe knowing what Emery is up to, why he took Wolf and Bear and all their harness stuff and disappeared off down the street.

Maroochy whines and stands, puts both paws on the windowsill and stares out into the dark. Emery must be coming, or Dad, she always knows when they're coming. At least I hope it's one of them and not some kind of trouble.

She pads over to the door and back to the window, stares out again. Me, even with my face pressed to the

15

glass, hands around my eyes to block out the firelight, I can't see him. I can make out the shape of parked cars, most of them dead with no electricity to make them run, and the houses opposite, but I can't see Emery.

Since the power went out last month, people have been stealing the solar lights from the poles. The city just keeps getting darker and darker.

Maroochy takes my elbow in her mouth, tugs at me to follow her to the door, but I can't see Emery.

There's shouts down the street. Men, shouting angry stupid things that men shout when their world is out of control and being the loudest is the only thing they know to do. Dad says when chaos hits, there's always a few people that go around trying to make things worse. People that think they're better off in chaos. But most try to make things better. And they're quiet, too busy fixing things to be noisy. The quiet many, Dad says. And when you hear the noise, don't forget about the quiet many.

A thin shape in a black hoodie squeezes into the dark shadows of a shop doorway across the street. Emery! Who else is that skinny? Emery is fourteen but he's not got round to growing yet, and looking at the size of Dad, maybe he never will. Me, I'm only ten but I'm the tallest ten-year-old I know, almost as tall as Emery. I guess I take after Mum, she's a different mum to Emery's.

The men are shouting at the people by the fire, and they all grab their pots, scurry back inside their houses, doors slamming. When the men pass the shop front opposite, Emery gets low and slides across the road to our place. A key clicks in the door downstairs. Maroochy pulls my hand, her warm mouth damp. I grab the backpack and run to the door of our flat, pull the backpack on before I kick out the board under the doorknob and slide back the bolt.

'Wait,' I whisper to Maroochy and she sits wriggling on her bum, moving closer to the door anyway, as I open it and peer out.

Emery has a tiny LED light between his teeth, and he's climbing up the outside of the staircase. The stairs are full of shopping carts and furniture he put there to stop people coming up the stairs, which they tried to do last night, so Emery said, 'That's it! We can't stay here!' Emery knows which shopping cart he can move easiest to get past, which those people bashing around downstairs last night didn't know about.

Nontha left last week to go stay in her sister's high-rise, so luckily we didn't have to rescue her. Alvie Moore is locked down tight and the stair barrier we made is

17

gonna help keep him safe. I told him about the barrier, yelling under his door. I told him we might be going soon when I took that book I wasn't allowed to read back. It was difficult to read anyway. I closed it when I got to a kid called Piggy saying, 'We got to do something.' Coz that's what Emery was saying over and over. 'We got to do something.'

'Ella,' Emery says around the tiny torch in his teeth.

Me and Maroochy run to him. He wraps his strong skinny arms around me, even though Maroochy's all up in his face licking him like she never thought she'd see him again. Me too, Roochy. Me too.

'Ella, run back to the bathroom and get that old lipstick of your mum's and write on the bathroom walls for Dad so he knows where we've gone,' Emery whispers.

'Where are we going?' I ask.

'Write, "Gone to Ma's",' he says. Then, while I'm trying to figure out how we get that far up country to his mum's place, he says, 'Write it on the mirror, write it on the tiles, then go to the window facing the street and write my ma's name there.' He pushes the little torch at me. 'Got it?' he asks. 'You remember my ma's name?'

I nod.

'Good girl,' he says, and I punch him in the arm, coz

18

I'm not five no more and he better not keep talking to me like I am.

But I take the torch and I do what I'm told. The lipstick, dark red, already in the pocket of the backpack, coz I was taking it, coz it's something of Mum's and it kind of smells like Mum, and it was the colour she wore when she went to her job at the power company eight months and seventeen days ago when I saw her last.

Torch between my teeth, I use the lipstick to write on the bathroom tiles, and on the window facing the street in big strong letters, 'CHRISTMAS', coz that's Emery's mum's real and actual name, but I turn the torch off before I go near the window, like Dad taught me. And I'm sad to be wasting all Mum's lipstick. I always thought she'd wear it again one day, in a world so different it seems from now, where people go out places wearing lipstick. But if it has to go, and everything goes, I know, I'm glad it's going so Dad and Mum can find us again. I kiss what's left of the tube of lipstick, write 'I ♥ U' on the wall and stand it up on the windowsill. This is Mum's house. She was happy here. Her lipstick should stay. And maybe when Dad comes back, if he hasn't found her, and he's sad to see us gone, maybe he'll see it here, and smell it and remember her too.

19

I run back to the door, turn on the torch to find the stairs. Maroochy is already down, dancing, her claws rattling on the tiles by the front door. Emery waves me to hurry to him.

He grabs me, his arms strong, so much like Dad, and pulls me over the handrail, over the side of the stairs, sets me clinging to the outside like him so I can climb down. On the floor, with Maroochy sucking air through her nose at the door edge, Emery takes the torch from my mouth and clips a lead to Maroochy's collar.

'Rooch,' he says all bossy. 'Quiet!'

Maroochy's bum hits the floor again, wriggling, ready to go, while Emery turns the torch off, leaving us all panting too loud in the pitch black. He cracks the door and looks up and down the street. Orange light from the fire, shiny in his dark eyes.

'Come on,' Emery whispers. 'They're busy with the fire. Stay close.'

'We should wait for Dad,' I say again. 'Just one more day.'

'We've done that,' Emery says. 'We've waited for him four one-more-days.'

Emery pulls my black hoodie up over my head. 'Keep your face covered, little white girl,' he whispers.

20

I grab the edges of the hood and pull it over my face, coz that's the whitest thing of all of us. We're dressed in black, even Roochy, and Emery has got nice brown skin like his mum, not pale like me and Dad.

We duck low and step out, me shutting the door behind us, coz old Alvie Moore is still living on the top floor, boards hammered across his door from the inside, waiting for an army.

The noisy men have taken over the fire, laughing and passing a bottle of something they're drinking, spraying out through their lips over the fire, making the flames leap towards them.

Between leaps of flames, we tiptoe through the shadows. Emery in front, bent down to Maroochy's head, his hand through her collar, me following along behind, a big handful of Roochy fur from her hip in my fist so I don't get lost in the dark, other hand holding my hood down on the fire side. I try to run smooth so the sardine cans in my backpack don't clunk together.

This is how we leave our home. Silent shadows in the dark. No goodbyes to nobody. No time to pack away what's left of what we own that we haven't already traded for food.

The men yelling and whooping make me think

21

they seen us, sets my heart smacking my chest, pulse thumping in my head, makes my feet feel heavy and slow, makes time stretch forever. But they don't see us. We make it past and to the other side of the bus. Emery stands straight, lets Maroochy run to the end of her lead, and takes my hand.

'It's all gonna be okay now, Bells,' he whispers. 'I got a plan.'

ALL OF US CROUCHING
IN THE DARK

'Where's Bear and Wolf?' I whisper, coz I'm hoping he didn't trade them along with my bickies. Bear and Wolf are family, and I lost too much family already.

'They're waiting for us, just outside the city,' Emery says, and I'm happier right away. Nobody's gonna pick on us with three big doggos by our sides.

'We're gonna go to Ma's,' he says.

'But she won't want the rest of us turning up,' I say, coz nobody wants more people or dogs to feed.

'She didn't want to live in the city, so far from her home, with her dad sick and her mum needing help, that's all,' Emery says. 'She loves me, and she's gonna love my little sister and our doggos, so shut up about that.'

'How do you know she's safe and still there?' I ask.

'They were farming mushrooms. Mushrooms are a fungus. The one thing we know is still growing. They'll still be there. And those caves Grandma uses are amazing, no one will ever find them. No one but me.'

'How we even gonna get there? You got a car?' I ask, but I don't think Emery can drive.

'Nah,' Emery says. 'We're not gonna travel by roads, anyhow. It's not safe, half the roads are blocked off. The dogs are gonna take us overland.'

'We're going mushing?' I ask. Emery and Dad are real good at dog-sledding on wheels, that's why we have three big malamutes in the first place.

But our mushing bikes are just big scooters we tie one or two dogs to, and I'm not sure I can manage to steer behind one of our big dogs without falling off. But I guess I'll have to learn. Because that's what Dad said when the food dried up and the city went wild. He said, 'The people who survive when the world turns upside down are the first ones who learn how to walk on their heads.' Which I'm thinking means, everything's different, and so I gotta try to be different to match it. I wish Dad was here.

'Yep, mushing,' Emery says. 'But I got a surprise. Wolf and Bear are taking care of it till we get there.'

I'm thinking it's my Anzac bickies, coz I'm starving, and I can't think of one single thing I want more right now.

Wait. There is one thing I want more. 'Dad?' I ask, and it can't be, coz I had to write where we were going in lipstick so Dad would know.

'Aww! Ella!' Emery says in big outward breaths like he's annoyed. 'If Dad had come back I'd be telling you right away. He's run into something, and we gotta go on without him for a while.'

'Is he dead?' I say, coz when someone's already annoyed, it's easier to ask the questions that will make them annoyed anyway.

'Ha!' Emery says. 'That man is made of steel poles held together with wire. You know that. Ain't nothing can kill our dad.'

I nod, say 'Yeah', but Emery's never had his mum just vanish, so he don't know how easy it is. One minute things are fine, and in a flash, they're all changed, and there are giant empty holes in your life. She phoned us a few times before the phones went out, to let us know she was 'Essential Personnel' and now employed by the

25

government to keep the power going, so she had to live on site at the power company, and she was safe behind 'tight security' so we didn't need to worry about her at all.

When the power went out, I said, 'Now Mum can come home!' Dad said it didn't work like that. She was probably working real hard to put it back on. But it didn't come back on. She didn't come home that week or the week after. So Dad went to get her.

'It'll be all right,' Emery says. He takes my hand and tows me down the city streets, the three of us ducking into gardens and doorways whenever we see people.

We get to the checkpoint for our area, set up last year to stop people from poor areas raiding the homes of rich areas, Dad said. He said that meant it was set up to keep us in. The gate is shut across the road, but the guard gate is left open and the guard hut is dark.

'No one's there,' Emery whispers, but we get down real low as we pass the guard house anyway, and scurry away into a suburb with bigger front gardens, some of them with huge security fences topped with barbed wire and warning signs stuck on the wire mesh.

One big house even has a man in a police vest and helmet sitting behind sandbags in the front yard, with a rifle resting on the sandbags like he's got his own little fort. I wonder if the rich kids who live in that house sleep cosy knowing they're never gonna get looted in the night.

Maroochy growls low and we turn the corner and find a group of people hooting and hollering outside a house. Emery pulls us back behind a hedge and we sit in someone's front yard, eating sardines from a can to keep Maroochy from barking, until they finish smashing up the house or whatever they're doing and move on.

The house we're in front of has big bars on the ground-floor window and barbed wire looped over the gate to the side. The curtains twitch, but no one yells at us to get back on the street. Maybe they're as scared as we are about all that noise going on around the corner. All of us crouching down in the dark trying not to be noticed.

A WHITE RIBBON
IN THE MOONLIGHT

Then we're back, moving quiet and silent through the dark streets. When we get to the gate to this suburb, it's not abandoned. It's lit up by solar street lights mounted on the top of a truck, over its open side. A crowd is in the light, pushing and shouting, trying to get through the gate and closer to the truck. Two men with rifles stand in front of boxes stacked up in the truck. Me and Emery stay back in the shadows, Emery hanging tight to Maroochy's head.

The gate's not guarded, but the truck on the other side is. And there's a couple of men in the crowd, shouting and taking money and lining people up. A woman appears from inside the truck and she's handing down cans of food, and I think maybe the government is delivering food parcels again, but we never had to pay before.

Emery nudges me and points at an opening in the fence on one side of the gate. 'Come on!' he whispers.

But I'm hanging back coz all those people have to do is turn and they'll see us!

Emery grabs me and tows me, and I duck low and run with him. But I want to stop and talk about this, not run. He's so busy keeping Maroochy moving quiet, he can't turn back and talk to me.

We get to the fence and drop down low.

A man yells, 'Gold! I said gold, not silver. Gold, diamonds or cold hard cash. If you haven't got it, go back and get it. Stop wasting our time!'

We squeeze through the gap in the fence, where the wire's been cut. Emery first, then Maroochy, then me, crouching again.

'April!' the shouty man calls into the truck. 'Three cans for this man!'

'No! A whole box. That ring is worth two grand, easy!' A man in a business shirt, sleeves rolled up, is leaning into the truck waving at the woman to give him more.

'Not to me, it's not. It's worth three cans. Take it

29

or leave it,' the shouty man says, and one of the men standing in the truck steps up and shoves a gun into the face of the business shirt man.

'Run now,' Emery whispers and pulls me up.

Behind me, the business shirt man shouts, 'This is unfair!' and the crowd agrees, yelling stuff about food being too expensive, and kids to feed, but me and Emery and Maroochy are back into the night, running down the street, and then a side street, and I hope Emery knows where we're going. The shouting crowd is far away but seems closer in the still night air. Then a crack rings out. It bounces off the walls of the houses around us and seems to come from everywhere, stopping my heart, making me gasp for air. Then another shot snaps off into the dark, sending me ducking like there's a bullet flying somewhere that might bounce off the walls like the echoes and get me.

Emery pulls us up against a hedge and we're staring back to the main road where the truck was. The truck roars and lights appear at the end of the road. The truck with the canned food races past the end of the street. Just a flash of a picture, like in a movie, the headlights pointing forwards, the driver's white face over the steering wheel, and the solar lights mounted on the roof of the truck. In that light, as the truck speeds on, the two men are still standing in the back, pointing their guns out like the crowd might be chasing them.

'It's okay,' Emery says.

'Did someone get shot?' I ask.

'Probably just warning shots,' he whispers. 'Hard to get money out of rich people if they's dead.'

He leads me and Maroochy on up the street and into a park where tents are pitched on the hard, bare ground, and people are gathered around a bonfire, sitting on scraps of ripped, old furniture. Where did these people come from? What did they leave that makes camping in a park seem better? How do they feel safe with just tents and bits of tin around them?

There's a cough and Emery throws himself around Maroochy's head. A man is standing under a tree in the dark ahead of us, just watching the people in the camp. Emery tugs my sleeve and pulls me down too. The three of us sitting silent in the shadows, watching the firelight dancing in the eyes of the man, standing, watching, like he's thinking evil fiery things.

What if he turns those fire eyes on us? I crawl back the way we came, one hand, then the other, then a knee, each finding the dirt, gently, silently, on and on, with

31

my mouth open, breathing softly, until there are bushes between me and that staring man.

I stand then, staying bent low so I'm still lower than the bushes, coz now I'm worried that the park is full of strange men standing, staring, in the pitch black of the trees. Ones I haven't even seen yet.

Emery and Maroochy arrive beside me. Emery takes my hand and wraps it around Roochy's collar, then he leads her on, back the way we came and then, slowly, a different way through the park. We stick close to the bushes, trying to be invisible, even though Maroochy is straining to tug us faster.

Emery pulls us through some bushes and stretching out in front of us is a white ribbon in the moonlight. A white concrete path, surrounded by trees, black against the dark grey of the sky. Water trickles in the distance, like there's a creek or a drain somewhere in the trees.

Emery doesn't let us walk on the path, he keeps us to the side of it, on the grass.

'Too noisy,' he says, but every now and then one of us steps on a stick anyway, and a crack rips into the night, telling the people in the dark we're here.

THE LIGHT IS NOT OUR FRIEND

My tongue's dry from breathing silently, and my stomach's tight. We're walking quick as we can when we get around a corner, and tiny white lights are bobbing in front of us further up the white path. I can't work out what it is. Then there's a whir. A whir that gets louder, like a thousand rubber moths flapping at once. It's tyres on concrete! It's bicycles!

Emery grabs my arm so hard it hurts. He pulls me away from the track, into the bushes. Someone hoots like they seen us, and the bikes chase us. Lights bounce around behind us as the bikes hit the rough ground, lighting up bushes and trees and logs. One bike cuts between me and

Emery. Me stumbling while pulled too hard. So Emery, never letting go of my arm, hauls me sideways over the front wheel of the bike, banging my legs, making me fall. Down into the leaves and dirt, the smell of it right in my face, dust in my throat. Then Emery's only got the sleeve of my black jumper and he's hauling on it, dragging me. Me trying to get up. Me hoping Emery never lets me go. Don't you dare let me go! You promised to keep me safe! I scramble, but I can't get my feet under me. Then someone behind me grabs my leg. I scream.

A bark, a growl, and a black blur leaps over me. Maroochy! Teeth snap on teeth, and the hand lets go of my leg.

'Argh!' he yells, and he sounds young. He's sliding back through the leaves on the ground, scuffling, and a bike chain clangs as he gets to his bike and pulls it back upright. The front bike-light brightens up the bushes back near the path. Rooch is growling in the gra, gra, gra, sound she makes when she's playing tug-of-war. She still has him. A hunk of pant leg maybe, a shoe.

Other bikes arrive, lights striping around, glaring, flashing over trees and us, tyres scraping, pedals rattling.

'What's happening?' someone asks. They most probably can't even see our black Roochy in these puddles of light.

34

'Help me!' the guy says, then grunts and struggles. Then he yells, 'Let's get out of here!' and Roochy barks. She's let him go.

'Rooch!' Emery calls and she's back, licking my face, letting me wrap my arms around her neck, then Emery's there, hauling me up, pulling me away. Breathing so fast, as he drags me and Roochy away through the night.

We run, banging into bushes, crashing through branches, sticks tangling in our legs, not caring about noise now...too scared to care.

Then Emery pulls me behind a tree. He holds his breath, me too, listening for bike tyres, the clang of a bike chain, voices. A night bird squawks nearby and I jump, grab at my thudding heart.

'You okay?' Emery says.

'Yeah,' I whisper.

'You always gotta be ready to run, Ella, always,' he says like I didn't. Like I wasn't moving fast as I could, soon as I saw it was bikes.

'You were pulling me awkward, and I—'

'You gotta keep up,' he says.

I shove him. I can't talk, coz I'm crying, and it's dark, so he don't have to know if I don't say anything in my cracked-up crying voice, but I did my best and I still

35

got grabbed, and now I'm terrified. What if it was more people? What if it was grown-ups, not just teenagers on bikes who are scared of dogs? What if someone had hurt Roochy? I breathe through my mouth so I don't sniff and let Emery know I'm crying, but I can't stop my hands from shaking.

'Let's keep moving.' Emery grabs my arm, finds my hand. He must feel the shaking. 'Baby Bell,' he says, using Dad's nickname for me, and squeezes my hand. 'It'll be okay.'

'I'm not a baby,' I say. I'm angry but not at Emery. I'm angry at me, for falling, for crying, for acting like a baby.

'Shh,' Emery says like he understands, he hugs me quick and strong with skinny arms like Dad does and it just makes me miss Dad more.

We pick our way carefully through the trees, looking for that white concrete ribbon, now just a dull path in the dark to lead us out of the city.

One of the solar lights over the bike path hasn't been stolen from its pole yet, but Emery don't let us walk through that circle of light, he makes us go way around it. The light is not our friend.

ON THE MOON

It seems like we walk through the whole night. My feet are heavy and sore and my legs ache, and still we walk on. Then the trees drop away from beside the path and we're walking on dirt in the open and the only lights and fires are little dots far, far away.

Emery stops. He turns into the darkness, onto rough ground, then tilts up at the stars like he's looking for something. Maroochy is sucking in air through her nose like she's searching for something too, then she lets out a long howl and somewhere in the darkness it's answered.

'Thanks, Rooch,' Emery says. She tows us faster then, up over a bare hill and behind some trees to a little shed.

She tows us right into two whining, panting, excited faces full of tongues and fur and bouncing like mad. Wolf and Bear! And there's more whining nearby. White shapes bounce on the ends of leads under a tree.

'Who's that?' I ask.

'Oyster and Squid,' Emery says.

'Tama's huskies?' I ask. 'You traded my bickies for more mouths to feed?' And I'm getting angry and hot about that, but Emery's not noticing at all in the dark.

'Yep. Tama and his brother got a boat and they're sailing to New Zealand. He says there's enough rain and good soil there for people to grow lots of veggies and stuff to feed pigs and keep them all fat and happy. He needed your bickies to stock up for the trip, for when they get bored of fish. He said we could go with them.'

'But you said not without Mum and Dad?' I ask, still steaming hot at him.

'Nah,' Emery says, and there's a smile in his voice. 'Tama's terrible at fishing. I said no in case he was just planning on eating our dogs, or you. A bit of meat on you.' Emery pokes me.

'No!' I say.

Emery laughs. 'Tama said it himself! He said his brother would most likely eat Oyster and Squid one night in a fit of hunger, so it's best if we take them up country where there's roos to eat. And look, look what else.'

Emery grabs my hand and shoves it on something cold and made of metal bars. I run my hands over it, hit webbing and tyres and handlebars.

'Oh,' I say. 'Is this Tama's big fancy cart?' Maybe this is worth my Anzacs.

'Yep. And I've got his tent and sleeping bags, and some pots and camping stuff, and a big old hunting knife, so we're all self-sufficient.' Emery sounds so proud to get this all sorted out for us.

'You and me and five big dogs,' I say, thinking it over as I go to say hello to Oyster and Squid, let them lick my hands. Maybe we're gonna be okay.

'Only problem is,' Emery says, 'I can't put the tent up in the dark, so maybe you can just sleep on the sleeping bag for a few hours? We need to get moving at first light, get away from the city.'

I take off my sneakers, climb into the sleeping bag that Emery gives me, and lie down on the rocky ground next to Bear, who doesn't mind my head on his back. With the ground so stony under my hip, I think I'll never sleep. I lie listening to Bear's heart beating and his breath going in and out, thinking how we've got a long way to go tomorrow and I gotta sleep a little bit, but scared to stop listening for footsteps in the dark, in case someone stumbles on us.

Then Bear's jumping up and the horizon is pink, and Emery is saying, 'Put your shoes on!'

I groan coz I'm too tired to wake up, and my mouth is too dry and old-fish flavoured to talk back. And Emery is ripping open cans of sardines and sliding out just three little sardines to each dog, licking oil off his fingers between dogs.

'They got a lot of running ahead of them this morning,' he's saying. 'We can go without food for a while, but they can't.'

I nod, I don't want more fish anyway, and pull on my shoes, roll up the sleeping bag, stow it back in the webbing sling of the cart, next to another sleeping bag and a little tent. There's a couple of two-litre bottles of water sitting there too, and I open one, heft it up, and guzzle a little. Maroochy licks her lips at me. Emery fed her first. She's the lead dog. She always gets fed first. There's a little metal pot in the cart so I pour some water into the pot and hold it for her to get a drink then go to Bear and Wolf and Oyster and Squid, making sure they've all had a drink.

40

The sky is getting lighter by the minute. The land shows itself to me, and I just stand and stare. I want to cry. It's so bare. Trees just growing out of dry dirt with a few scrubby weeds. No grass. I've seen all the little dead lawns, I've seen the dead parks, I watched the news showing the wheat turn red then black, but I haven't been out of the city since the grass started dying and this, all this land, all this dead grey and red dirt, stretching on and on over the hills, looking like a desert or the moon, it's not right.

WHICH ONE OF US
IS ON THE BEST PATH

Emery's getting the harnesses sorted out in front of the cart.

'Oyster and Squid know this cart, so I'll set them up right next to it, and then Rooch will have Bear and Wolf between her and Oyster and Squid,' he says. 'Huskies are all about speed, and Bear and Wolf should be closer to the cart to get it rolling, since malamutes are all about the muscle, but that's just not going to work yet. We'll just have to run and push it off like Tama used to.'

Bear and Wolf are always so laid back, letting Roochy be the leader, happy to be like little puppies around her, but Oyster and Squid got their own ideas about who the leader is in their family, and it ain't none of us. But after the sardines, they look happy to do anything Emery asks.

I turn to scanning the houses up on the hillsides for signs of life. One has dumped cars all around it, like a little fort. I don't think they can see us down here in the still dark.

I clip the dogs to the gang line one by one after Emery straps them into their harnesses. They're bouncing and yipping, happy to be getting ready to go for a run, but they know it's not time yet, and they're almost busting trying to keep a lid on it.

Emery stands on the back of the cart, yelling for Maroochy to pull the line out, 'Line, Rooch! Line!' Then he opens one arm to let me stand up on the step in front of him, while Maroochy prances like a pony, testing the line, lifting it off the dirt, ready to go.

'Maroochy! Mush! Hike! Hike!' he yells, letting the brake go and pushing off with one foot. Maroochy leaps forwards, throws herself into the harness, pulling the gang line straight. Bear and Wolf leap after her, and Oyster and Squid, yipping like puppies, follow them and we're off, along the bike path, wind flying at my eyes, whipping my hair.

'Emery!' I yell, coz it's too fast. The cart is just a giant

43

tricycle really. A big knobby tyre wheel at the front, and two smaller wheels on the back. A set of handlebars that Emery gets to steer and brake with, leaving me just clinging to the frame. Our gear sits just behind the front wheel guard, in that triangle, and it's bouncing about like mad, with only the netting and some bungee cords stopping it from bouncing out. All I got to stand on is a little platform skinnier than a step, with rubber tread on it.

'They'll slow down,' Emery says. 'May as well run fast while the path is smooth and straight!'

After a while of hanging onto the metal bar in front of me with both hands, knuckles white as paper, face scrunched up, I figure out we're not gonna crash or tip, and when we get to a bit of a bend in the path, and Emery shouts, 'Haw!' and Maroochy heads left and we make it around nice and smooth, I relax off a bit. Maroochy is paying attention to Emery. She won't let us crash.

We race for ages before the dogs slow to an easy run. The bike path follows a road for a while and Emery is looking up and down it, like he don't know what he'll do if he sees a car, and then there is a car. It sneaks up on us coz it's electric and just a whir of wheels. Before Emery can do anything, a red car with a big black solar roof is on the road behind us, driving flat out. Fast, like someone stole it. Fast, like someone needs to get a lot of distance from the city before it goes flat. Too fast for anyone driving to be looking at a dog cart on the bike path beside the road. Except there's a kid in the back with his face pressed to the window, and he looks right in my eyes. Everything so clear in the early morning light, him in his car with his parents driving him out of the city, and me on a dog cart, getting out of the city too, twisting my head, following the car, not wanting our eyes to break their hold, coz we're the same, him and me, scared to our bones, running to who knows where. But the car is too fast and the boy has to bounce up into the back window to keep staring, and the dogs pull us away from the road, following the railway line instead, on a bike path built for city cyclers to get out of the city for nice daytrips.

The kid's still staring as our paths separate, as he stays on the road and we head away into the bare countryside. And I wonder, watching that little red car get smaller and smaller, which one of us is on the best path.

WE STAND TOGETHER

The sun heats up and climbs higher and higher, and the dogs slow down, trotting along with mouths open and tongues lolling. The path climbs up and runs on top of where railway tracks used to run back in the old days. The wood and steel's been torn up now and turned into smooth concrete bike paths for serious bike riders.

'Thing is,' Emery says over the whir of our wheels on concrete, 'all these old lines lead to little country towns like they always did.'

I nod. 'We wanna stay out of towns,' I say.

We mostly just wanna stay away from people, I guess. People who might steal our cans of fish, and maybe eat our dogs. People who've got guns to shoot them.

The dogs are really panting and Emery slows them down, and we get off and walk beside them for a while. The sun is burning the top of my head now, and my stomach is aching of empty.

'This concrete's no good for their paws,' Emery says. 'And they can't run in the heat. But we gotta put some distance between us and the city real quick, so we need to stay on it a bit longer. Gotta get bush so we can find them some roos and stuff to eat.' He adjusts the knife in its holder on his belt, and this is like a different Emery to the one I know. This is bush-kid Emery.

There's an old railway bridge ahead, built when people had time to make bridges look nice. The sides are like concrete balustrades and it has big pillars underneath holding it up, built from great rectangles of bluestone stacked up, making arches. There's shade and cool water down there, so without Emery and me even saying a word to each other, we know we're gonna rest up there for a while.

Emery leads Maroochy off the track, down to the creek, with the other dogs following and me walking behind, holding the cart brake, so it doesn't run forwards and bang into the dogs.

47

Emery unclips Maroochy and sends her down to the creek for a drink first, then lets off Bear and Wolf, who trot after Maroochy.

'Don't let those two off,' Emery warns, coz Squid and Oyster still aren't part of our pack, and we don't want them disappearing on us or getting into a fight with Maroochy. 'I'll come get them,' he says.

He clips leads to both their collars and wraps them around his hand, while I shove the cart down towards some bushes so anyone up on the path can't see it.

Roochy sets up growling real low and staring under the bridge, and Wolf and Bear stop splashing around and look what's set Rooch off.

There's some scuffling under the bridge. Emery back-pedals towards me, dragging Oyster and Squid with one hand, waving me down with the other.

'Behind the bushes,' he whispers, like he's worried for me. He shoves the leads at me and pushes me off to the bushes. But he's ducking away and running forwards, clicking his fingers to call Rooch off quietly. She's not backing down, her hackles are up on her shoulders and her head is real low, fangs showing. Bear and Wolf though, they're pleased to be told what to do, and they scramble out of the creek to Emery, who's got his back against the bank beside the path. With them behind him, he creeps closer to the bridge trying to look under it without being seen.

White-sneakered feet are scrambling back behind a pillar, slipping on the rocks. Someone's sitting in the cool under the bridge, like we want to. They'll have seen me, even if they can't see Emery now. I run after Emery, taking the dogs with me. No way I'm letting him face people alone! I'm almost as big as him. Almost.

JUST ANOTHER COW

Squid and Oyster are panting and whining, bouncing, all excited about Maroochy still growling and creeping forwards, like it's a game. Even though they're hot and stinky sweaty from all that running.

Emery's giving me 'make them shut up' looks as well as jerking his head to tell me to get away, as well as waving one hand to keep Bear and Wolf behind him, and silent snapping his fingers to get Rooch to come to him. But he needs to be watching out for the people under the bridge, so he gives up telling me what to do and creeps forwards, hand on his knife, still trying to get Rooch's attention without shouting at her. No way I'm backing off. He'd never leave me to face anything alone.

There's more scuffling from under the bridge. Rooch lunges forwards, growling and barking like she's launching a war.

Squid and Oyster leap after her, their leads burning through my hands, my feet sliding on gravel, trying to stop them dragging me towards the bridge. Then I'm just busy hanging onto them without face-planting as I slide past Emery and out into the open.

The person makes a break from under the bridge, and it's a woman, pushing a three-wheel stroller, bumping over rocks, and a little toddler clinging to the handrail, eyes round and bottom lip trembling at a massive black dog racing at her. The woman leaps in front of the stroller. I run flat out, dogs towing me at Maroochy.

'Rooch! No!' I shout.

And Maroochy has the sense to slow, coz there's nothing scary about the woman except the look on her face as she turns and wraps herself over the toddler.

And then me and Oyster and Squid are on top of Maroochy, me grabbing her collar as she turns her protective growling on poor Squid, who scrambles away. Rooch drags me with her. I can't let her go, or she'll bite Squid. Then Emery is in the middle too, and Rooch only

51

gets a mouthful of pale Squid hair before she minds his yelling and backs off. And Oyster's coming in all growling to protect Squid a bit too late, and Emery turns his attention to sorting her out.

While this is all going on, the woman is halfway up the track on the other side of the bridge bumping the stroller so bad the toddler bangs her head on the side of it and starts wailing. The woman's looking over her shoulder like we're wild and dangerous, and I think we kind of are, with these new dogs complicating things.

Bear and Wolf, seeing that everything is under control, are galloping about, sniffing at us to smell us calming down, and running after the woman to sniff her and see what she's up to. She shoos them off and keeps bumping her screaming baby up the track. It can't be easy, coz the stroller is loaded down with bags of belongings, but she makes it to the path and across the bridge and starts running.

'Wait!' I say. 'Are you okay? Do you need water or something to eat?'

'Let her go,' Emery says.

'But it's hot. What if she didn't have time to fill her water bottle?' I ask.

'Never tell anyone we have food,' Emery says and

shoves Oyster away so there's a big gap between her and Maroochy.

'It's only cans of fish,' I say.

'Yeah, well, they'll find that out after they shoot us, won't they?'

'What do you mean?'

'What if that woman runs into some mean people further up the path, and they grab her baby and she tells them there's a couple of kids under the bridge who offered her food? What do you think those mean people do next?'

'Oh,' I say.

'That woman's doing the right thing. Stay away from other people. Mind your own business. Get out of the city.'

'So we can't be nice to anyone?' I ask.

'It's a new world, Els. You can't trust people like you used to.'

The wailing of the toddler is getting quieter and quieter as the woman runs away.

'But we're not different,' I say. 'There's gotta be people like us who are still nice and caring.' I don't think Dad meant, when he said we had to learn to walk on our heads, that we needed to be worse people.

'Let's hope they're the only ones we run into, then,' Emery says as he pushes Oyster and Squid's leads into my hand and pulls Maroochy away back to the creek. We both know that's too much to hope for, coz we've already seen the gangs of people in the city who just take what they want.

I wade into the creek, towing Oyster and Squid, and get down on hands and knees and drink as much of the water as I can. It doesn't matter if I get my clothes all wet, coz they're already wet from sweat, and I'll dry out.

I'm nervous now about being under the bridge and that woman telling people we're here, like Emery said. But the dogs need rest and it's too hot to have their paws up there on the concrete. So after Oyster and Squid have drunk and cooled themselves off in the creek, I tie them to a bush in the shade of the bridge and sit down with them, and the other dogs stretch out on the cool creek mud in front of us and sleep through the heat of the day. Emery must be nervous, too, coz he organises the cart and gang lead, ready to go, and won't sit down with me and the dogs and rest until he's checked every wet harness each dog is still wearing, each paw to make sure they're okay, and made sure every dog is ready to clip back in.

When the sun gets lower, we all fill up on water

once more and Emery opens another couple of cans of sardines, and the dogs get three each and me and Emery get one each. We head off again, the sun low in our faces, one tiny sardine in our bellies to stop us from starving.

The dogs are less excited this time and the fierce gallop slows straight away to a trot. We keep going till the sun goes down and the sky is just a glow of light behind far-off hills and it's almost too dark to see the concrete path. We find somewhere off to the side, under some trees, the dirt all smoothed out and hard from sheep or cows sheltering from the sun there, way back before they all got eaten, back when this was paddocks of grass.

It's water from the pot for everyone and more sardines, which I would hate but I'm too starving. Then we lay out the tent and unroll sleeping bags on top, and with dogs either side of us, I feel safe, and I think about Dad out there somewhere, and has he found Mum yet. Did he already come back and knows we've gone?

When I close my eyes, I keep seeing all those grey and red-brown dry paddocks rolling by. Only weeds and prickles. No grass anywhere. All that dead dirt.

Dad said he never realised before how much grass he used to eat. Bread and rice, and noodles, and corn, and meat, and dairy, and even his beer, all made of grass. He said he was just another cow, about to starve. Then he shook his head and looked at me like he shouldn't have said that.

'How did we get so that most of our food came from one kind of plant? All our eggs were in one basket,' he said to me, but not really expecting an answer.

I said, 'Don't worry, Dad. Baskets are made of grass and eggs came from wheat-eating chooks, so we won't do that again!'

He wrestled me and called me cheeky and rubbed my short-clipped hair for that.

I smile, thinking about him, and fall asleep with him so close.

THIS ISN'T THE OUTBACK

It's real cold in the night and I lie staring up through black branches at the stars. I wish we'd set up the tent but the dogs huddle closer and, soon enough, the low morning sun creeps in under the trees and warms my back. I'm real tired but Emery is up and packing the cart right away, so I have to crawl out of the sleeping bag and go find somewhere to pee. Then I just stand around on the bare dry dirt in the low sun and stare at the naked land.

In the cracks of the dirt at my feet there's a few weeds trying to take over, stems flat and pink and tiny green round leaves.

I can't stop this idea that over the hills somewhere, there are fields of green grass dotted with sheep. Wheat fields shining yellow in the sun. That somehow, if we just run far enough, we'll get there. But I saw on the news, before they stopped the TV stations, that there's no grass anywhere in the whole world no more. No rice in Asia even, with all those people needing it. No maize in Africa, and no corn in America. And no way to grow enough potatoes, pumpkins and cabbage to replace them in time. I think that's why they stopped showing us the news. They didn't want us to be scared.

The trees there are out here look thirsty and dry when there's no grass around them, and even in this hardly-anything light, the red bare dirt is hot to look at. It hasn't stopped patches of pale grey prickles from taking hold though, and other weeds, spindly and dry.

Rooch, Wolf and Bear are all sniffing around a group of trees and looking up like maybe there's a possum up there, as Emery gives Oyster and Squid some water and straps them into the cart.

Then he calls the other dogs over one by one and gives them some water too and straps them in. There's no fish for any of us this morning. I think we're down to just two cans and we've still got a long way to go.

There's a far-off roar and rumbling and I run to the cart behind the trees and pull the dogs back, tuck in behind the tree trunks, help Emery to keep the dogs quiet by hanging onto Oyster and Squid's noses and pulling their heads in tight to my belly, covering their ears with my elbows, whispering, 'Shush, shush, shush now.'

Three motorbikes speed past on the bike path, the roar of them so loud, echoing around this empty land, bouncing off bare hills, that it surrounds us and thumps into my heart, sets it rumbling like it never knew its own beat, and the dogs hear my heart gone mad and whimper and pull away. Maroochy growls like she's a great big motorbike, and I think the riders will hear her. But the bikers and their rumbling-bellied bikes speed on by.

Emery shakes his head. 'We need to get further out, real quick,' he whispers. 'This is just a daytrip from the city for people like that.'

And I don't know for sure what he means when he says 'people like that' but three guys on motorbikes probably aren't out for a fun ride like in the old days. They're probably looking for food, and most people don't want to give up what food they got.

So we set up the cart again and lead the dogs back to the bike track. And both of us stand there looking along it. Looking for the tail lights of those motorbikes. Emery is standing, holding Roochy's neck fur with one hand, rubbing at the back of his own neck with the other, like he does when he's worried.

He tells Rooch to sit, and comes back to the cart, hauls out the map and studies it, running his finger along a dotted line.

'Probably,' he says slowly. 'Probably they won't be back for a while. The nearest town is maybe half an hour away for them.'

I nod. 'We should hear them before they see us,' I say, but as we set off again, my ears burn to hear that rumble bouncing off the hills.

Almost an hour, maybe, we're running, tyres of the cart muttering on the concrete, my ears straining like mad. Then concrete changes to pressed shell rock, which puffs up under the claws of the dogs. The sun is up and the dogs are panting, and we go almost half an hour more, then Emery calls, 'Easy! Easy, Roochy! Haw!' and Roochy looks back, to check he's serious and slows the other dogs and pulls them off the track, into a wide flat paddock.

'We should go overland,' Emery says to me, and we head off across a dusty, dry paddock that maybe once had sheep or cows but now is just bare dirt and prickles, weeds, fence posts leaning, wire broken or gone, gates left open anyway.

We're moving slower than on the bike track, winding through the paddocks, the cart bumping along, but I'm feeling better that we're here, where nobody goes, dipping down between small hills, behind blocks of trees so we're kind of sheltered from the world passing by on tracks and roads. We're away from men on motorbikes. We're away from people, and I'm thinking that people are scary now, scary like snakes. I don't know if they're gonna attack us or run away like that woman with the baby did. But I'm hoping they're gonna run away. Always run away.

We stop and rest under some trees when the sun gets too high in the sky. Emery opens the last two cans of fish and shares it out to the dogs. None for us. He looks at me like I might argue as the last sliver of fish slides down Squid's throat, not even chewed, just gulped whole and Squid straight away looking for more, licking oil from Emery's fingers, so excited.

'We don't get anywhere if they can't run,' I say, like I believe there's food somewhere out there where we're headed, but really, I think maybe me and Emery are just gonna starve.

I drink a gulp of water to fill the ache in my belly, and pour water into the pot for the dogs, then we all sleep the warm afternoon away in a pile together in the shade. I'm so tired with no food to keep me going. So tired.

I wake up scared when I hear motors and shouting and see Emery and Rooch standing and the other dogs with their ears pointing straight up. I'm not used to hearing motors in old cars, coz I been living in the city full of electric cars. It fades like it's people driving away and shouting at each other.

Emery shakes his head and sits back down.

When Emery wakes me again to keep going, I'm still too tired to wake up properly, so I just sit on the standing board of the cart, with my feet in the webbing basket, and watch the dirt slide under us as we head across the country once more. When the sun gets low in the sky and the air gets cooler, I wake up and struggle to my feet. We're running alongside a road. Not a sealed road though, just two tracks in shingle, and there's something way ahead in the road.

Emery takes us way around it, out to some trees and a dip in the land. And when we're nearly level with the thing in the road, I make out a bridge, collapsed in the middle and on the other side sits a big old horse truck parked crossways on the road, with a sign on it saying 'Road Closed'. A couple of old cars and some tractor ploughs and other farm stuff make a massive roadblock that no cars or motorbikes are going to get past in a hurry.

Once we go down the dip, cross a creek and climb up again on some old sheep track, looking back, there's a couple of men sitting there up against the horse truck, on white plastic chairs working on getting a little fire going between them, dropping bits of cardboard or something on it, and chatting and laughing. A couple of rifles sit propped up against the chairs.

I duck lower on the cart and Emery takes it back down inside the dip.

'I don't think they saw us,' he says.

I nod. I feel like we're a long way from any highways here but still there's a lot of people and houses around. This isn't the outback, even surrounded by all this bare red dirt. This was once all farmland and maybe people have stayed on to grow potatoes or something. After all, they'd be better off than we were in the city, waiting on food deliveries that ain't never coming.

THERE'S GOATS
UP THE HILL

We stay in the dip and eventually it curves around back towards the shingle road, so we go alongside that again for a while.

There's a house ahead sitting at the end of a drive, surrounded by trees. Out to one side there's rows of green plants and a few big squares of green. But it can't be grass, can it?

'Do you think anyone's there?' I ask as we get closer.

'It's got fruit trees,' Emery says, and he sucks in his lips and swallows. For his small size, he's always been a big eater, so he's probably even hungrier than me. We both want some fruit. But what if someone's there?

There's a fence around the fruit trees, and when the dogs trot us around the corner of the fruit tree fence to the back, there's an old woman in an apron sitting there, milking a goat. The goat bleats out a warning and the woman jumps up.

'Woah!' Emery says to Maroochy and jumps off and runs to hold her head.

'It's a couple of kids and a pile of dogs!' the woman calls as she stares at us.

A man steps out of the trees then. He's got a gun under his arm and he's wearing a chequered shirt in grey and red. A bucket with some fruit in it swings in his hand, and he looks us up and down.

'Well,' he says, 'what's this contraption?'

Emery says, real quick, 'It's a mushing cart, sir. Like they use in Alaska, but with wheels. We didn't mean to be on your land without permission.'

'You gave us a fright, but it's all right, kid. Most of it's not good for much now anyway,' the man says. 'How did you get past the roadblock?'

'We're not using roads, we're travelling overland. Just passing through. On our way to my mum's place,' Emery says.

'Where's she live then?' the man asks.

'Up country, sir,' Emery says all vague.

'Where's your parents?' the woman asks.

'My mum's up country,' Emery says again. 'Dad's following us up here, maybe a day behind.'

I look at Emery saying that like it's a real thing. I hope it's a thing that will happen.

'We're just wondering if we can camp somewhere near here, down at the creek maybe, to rest the dogs and catch them some eels to eat. Maybe if there's still some roos about, or possums, you wouldn't mind if we killed them to feed the dogs?'

'Kid, I can't kill those sickly roos fast enough,' the man says. 'They're all skin and bone, living off just weeds, help yourself.'

'Ted, they can stay in the house, we've got spare rooms and plenty of food,' the woman says.

And the idea of sleeping in a bed and having a shower and eating good food makes me smile.

'No,' Emery says, wiping the grin off my face. 'We'll be fine down by the creek. The dogs are too noisy anyway.'

'But—' I say.

Emery shakes his head at me.

'Well, wait here and I'll get you something to eat from the house,' the woman says and hurries towards the back steps.

The man, Ted, holds out the bucket of apples and plums. 'Want some of these?' he asks.

'Yes, please,' I say. I jump off the cart and hurry to him, take an apple and two plums.

'Take more,' he says, hoisting the bucket at me. 'I was just gonna give them to the goats anyway.' And I fill the front of my T-shirt with three apples and a whole pile of plums and take them back to my backpack on the cart.

'We got nothing to trade, sorry,' Emery says.

'Don't you worry,' Ted says. 'We've got fruit coming out our ears. Only so many preserving jars we can fill. Good to see it not going to waste.'

'Thank you,' Emery says. 'You know there's more people heading out of the city, looking for food. And they're mean-looking.'

'We've seen them. They've been here a few times, and we've banded together with the other farmers and chased them off. We're off the main roads,' Ted says. 'And we take turns at watching the roadblocks.'

'We got around the roadblock. Don't you have any place you could move to out of sight from the road?' Emery says. 'Someplace hidden?'

'Yes, it's almost coming to that,' Ted says, nodding

slowly like he's thought of moving already. Then he smiles at the woman coming across from the house with a couple of plastic containers. The first seems to be full of baked potatoes and pumpkin but the second is a big square of bright white stuff, and I think it's cheese! White goat cheese! I can't hardly believe it. It's been so long since we've seen any dairy. I just want to rip it open and sink my teeth into it.

'Oh!' I say, both hands reaching for it. 'Thank you!'

'We're doing real well out here,' the woman says. 'Got the root vegetables in early. Enough for us and a few goats and to trade with neighbours, and the fruit from the orchard, a couple of patches of clover, weeds, and turnips for the goats, and the veggie patch and we're all set to ride this thing out, till the scientists come up with a way to get rid of the fungus. Are you sure we can't offer you beds for the night?'

'No,' I say. 'We'll be okay down at the creek.'

Emery jumps in with, 'Probably we'll move on at first light. We don't want to wake you up.'

She nods, and I stow the plastic containers in my backpack and take out a couple of plums, coz I just have to eat something, right now, even though my mouth is watering for that cheese.

68

'Thank you,' I say again. 'Thank you so much.'

Emery waves and climbs up onto the cart behind me. 'Mush!' he calls to Maroochy and we set off again, across the bare farm, skirting around a giant potato patch and then on down a rough old tractor track towards a creek that just looks like a wobbly line of green trees, cutting through empty red dirt. As we get closer to the banks there are wandering weeds, trying to cover the ground like they want to own it. One is stretching out grey stems across the ground and has flat grey leaves, the other has stems red as the dirt, and tiny green buds of leaves like it's trying to stay hidden. Maybe it knows there's goats up the hill.

Emery checks over his shoulder again and again, and we go further and further along, not just down to the creek where he said we were going, and it seems he don't trust the old farmers.

'They seem real nice,' I say to him.

'Yeah. Seem,' he says.

'I think they were nice. I'd have liked a real bed, and a big breakfast.'

'For all you know they were fattening you up.'

I elbow Emery in the stomach. I don't want to hear stupid jokes about me getting eaten no more.

BACK TO
THE OLD WAYS

The sun gets lower and lower, and finally Emery points to a flat bit of sand tucked into a bank behind a few scrubby bushes, stopping the dogs.

'No one will see us there,' he says. He stumbles across the creek rocks and stomps about while I wait with the dogs, hanging onto the brake of the cart.

'It's sandy over here,' he calls, 'this will be soft to sleep on.'

There's a rustle in the bushes beside him and a small kangaroo breaks cover, leaps out, crosses the creek, stumbles, and bounds away in front of the dogs. Not only is it small, it's skinny. So skinny.

I yell, 'Woah!' just as Maroochy leaps after it.

Wolf and Bear yelp and follow. They're too hungry, there's no stopping them. The cart lurches forwards, all the dogs now, their mushing job forgotten, all trying to be the ones to bring down that roo.

I'm clinging to the cart as it bounces, dragged, coz I got the brake on. I can't steer it and brake, but I can reach the tag for the emergency release. I can set the dogs free of the cart. My fingers close around the red tag just as the cart tips, and me and the tent and the backpack full of fruit hit the dirt. Dirt in my face, scraping my elbow, the cart slamming into the side of my head, but I yank hard on that tag and the cart grinds to a stop. Yelping dogs take off without me, all still tied to the gang line.

'Ella!' Emery slides to a stop as I sit up, spitting out dirt, then twist my arm to see my bloody elbow. He grabs my shoulder.

'I'm okay,' I say.

He gives my shoulder a squeeze, grabs the knife in its leather holder from the pouch at the top of the cart and chases after the tangle of yelping, growling dogs.

There's a squeal as the roo goes down, then a growling scuffle breaks out, dust and teeth snapping as the dogs all want a piece and Emery yells, 'Drop it!' and wades into that mess, hauling Oyster and Maroochy apart by the neck fur, and all the dogs quit growling, except for Oyster, who really wants her piece of roo, right now. And that poor roo, it's not dead. It's still squealing. I cover my ears.

'Sit!' Emery yells again, his boot on the weak struggling roo, and four bums hit the dirt, and finally Oyster's goes down too.

Emery cuts the roo's throat. Quick and strong, like he knows how. I stand up, smack at the dust all over me, and limp over there. I'm glad it's not hurting or hungry anymore, poor roo.

As the roo bleeds to death, Emery releases each dog from the gang rope and moves each one to sit further apart, and away from each other.

He cuts the roo into lots of pieces. A whole thigh for Maroochy first coz she's the boss, then a forearm each for Wolf and Bear, and a lower leg each for Oyster and Squid to keep them still and chewing. He slices the other thigh into bits, hunks of roo with not much meat under the fur at all, and delivers a piece each to the four waiting dogs, then he guts the roo, it all spilling out onto the dirt, cuts the head off, chucks it outside the circle, the heart in one direction, the liver in another, the carcass apart from the spilled guts.

'There,' he says. 'They should be able to sort out who gets what, without fighting.' He collects up the gang rope and we go back and right the cart, repack all the stuff and carry it across the creek to behind the bushes on the sand.

We sit down and eat the cheese right away. Soft and creamy and salty, it gums up the roof of my mouth. Maybe heaven tastes like this. My stomach crawls up my throat to get to it, even if my mouth wants to go on tasting it forever. Cheese. I've forgotten what it tasted like and I never had goat cheese before, but I'm pretty sure cheese never tasted this good.

'Can't let it go off,' Emery says, and scoops two fingerfuls more out of the plastic pot and wipes them on his tongue. Shoves the pot at me.

I swallow finally and scoop the rest into my mouth and hold it there.

Emery takes the container back and licks it out, just like Maroochy.

'You go down to the creek and wash your elbow and face,' he says. 'I'll set up the tent.'

The creek water stings the graze on my elbow but I ignore it. There's no point whingeing when there's no one around with a bandaid or anything to help anyway. I fill the water bottles, and then go and sort the fruit into piles. The stuff that bruised when the cart tipped over has to be eaten, before the bruises taste bad, but that only leaves one apple and two plums for tomorrow, which I put back in the pack.

Emery and I crawl into the tent, door flap open, sit on the sleeping bags and eat the bruised fruit and the potatoes Ted and his wife gave us. The dogs find us, one by one, slinking back to sit near the tent and gnaw on bones. They stare at the other dogs, and get up and move, bones in their mouths, when another dog comes close. Oyster shows her fangs at the other dogs. Squid, Wolf and Bear just slink away like they don't want any arguments.

'They're all so hungry,' I say.

'I think we should just rest here tomorrow. The dogs are too thin to run day after day. We're too tired. And it seems like it's a safe place. If we can catch some eels or another roo, it'll be good for us all.'

Maroochy comes back to the camp last. She hasn't brought her bone. Maybe she's buried it somewhere.

'I'm gonna go for a quick look around,' Emery says.

'I'll come,' I say.

Emery piggybacks me across the creek so my boots

don't get wet again, and we climb to the top of a small hill nearby. It's so dark now I'm tripping on lumps in the dirt I can't see. There's just a bit of light left above in the sky. The five dogs trot after us and point their noses high and into the breeze. The farmhouse of the old people sits in the distance and there's light showing in one of the windows.

'They're so stupid,' Emery mutters. 'They stick out like a lighthouse.'

'Maybe they know no one can see them from a main road?' I say.

'Were those three bikers travelling on a main road?' Emery asks.

'Ted has a gun.'

'Maybe those people in the old cars had three guns. You remember what Dad said?'

'When the world turns upside down, the ones that survive are the first ones who learn to walk on their heads,' I say.

'Yep. Those people are still walking on their feet, thinking the world will flip right way up any day.'

'Maybe it will.'

'If someone makes a grass that can grow, how long before they make enough seeds to send to Australia? We're on the bottom of the world here, Ella. There's millions of starving people in Asia and America and Europe who are gonna be getting those seeds first, then how long before cows and sheep get brought back? There's no end to this anytime soon if we're waiting for help. They said the outback grasses are okay, so there's still healthy roos and emus out there.'

'What if everyone in the cities starts heading outback?'

Emery laughs. 'Most people will be too scared to do that. Most people will be clinging to their houses and their old lives.'

'Scared to try walking on their heads?' I ask.

'Yep,' he says. 'Ba harvested lots of seeds from the land and has been growing the old grasses. Our people been managing those grasslands and keeping the kangaroos near and healthy for thousands of generations. With that and Mum's mushrooms, we'll be eating fine once we get there, and maybe we'll have enough grass to share with the farms around us and then the rest of the state and then the whole country.'

I don't know much, but I know this whole country is too huge for Emery's grandad to save it all.

VEHICLES DRIVING OFF INTO THE NIGHT

We sleep in the next day, right through till midday. We're safe here, tucked away. The dogs are fed, and we've been fed, and I guess we were all real tired. Emery sharpens sticks with his knife and we lie around the creek trying to stab eels, but they turn out to be sneakier than us, and we go to bed with just water in our bellies. The dogs have their bones to chew, so they spend the evening trying to chew those to a pulp.

'I'll get up early and go hunting,' Emery says. 'And if that don't work, maybe we can ask Ted for more potatoes?'

'Yeah,' I say, glad we have a plan for food tomorrow.

We're fast asleep, me, Emery, five warm hairy dogs

around us, pinning my feet down. I'm dreaming of soft white cheese dripping down my T-shirt, and no matter how many times I slurp it back up, it just keeps dripping. Then Maroochy jumps up, stepping on my legs and growling. Emery is awake in a second, lunging for her, hanging on, saying, 'Shh!'

Maroochy keeps up her growling and over her noise there's far-off shouts and a loud 'Crack!' splits the night. I sit up too then. It's too dark to see, but Emery hauls up the zipper on the tent anyway, and there is something to see. Over the rise, back towards the farmhouse, there's a red glow. Like there's a fire over the hill. More shouting.

'We have to help them!' I say, thinking their house has caught fire.

'Shh!' Emery says, and he slaps Maroochy's head. It makes her jump. She stops growling. She's not used to being slapped.

We're all listening now. Men shouting, more than one.

'We have to help them!' I whisper.

'Nothing we can do,' Emery whispers back. 'We're two kids and a pile of dogs.'

'You've got a knife,' I say.

'To kill roos for food. To wave at someone if they try

to hurt us. Not to go fight a one-man war.'

He's right. I know he's right. I don't want him to go out there really.

'I'm going to see what's going on, you keep the dogs quiet,' he says.

'No!' I say 'I'll come too.'

'If we both go, the dogs will howl. You stay here!' He slides out of the tent and zips it closed behind him with Maroochy snorting and scratching at the zipper where he left.

'No, Rooch,' I say and pull her back. 'Wait.'

She yowls and complains in a grumble.

Emery is in his bare feet, silent across the sand, then splashing through the creek, then no sound. No sound except shouting in the distance.

It's hard to hear with five heavy-panting dogs. I dunno what they're shouting about, but the hair on my head stands up, like on the dogs' necks. Maybe I don't want to know.

Emery is gone too long. Any time for me alone is too long, but this feels like half the night goes by. Then Rooch starts whining and snorting at the zipper again. Water splashes in the creek. I don't know how she knows.

'It's me!' Emery whispers, and then he's unzipping

79

and crawling back through the tent flap with five dogs trying to lick his face.

'What's happening?' I whisper.

'It's too late,' he says. 'The house is gone. I dunno what happened to them. We'll wait till the sun's up and go look.'

I lie back down, dragging one of the dogs with me. Hard to know which one in the dark. The dogs seem calmer now that Emery has checked the noise out, they lie down and soon they're snoring, but I'm lying there listening to Emery's breath not regular like a sleeping person, and car doors slamming way back at the farmhouse, and vehicles driving off into the night.

Then it's light, and the zipper goes up and dogs bound off into the morning sun through the tent flap. I sit up and rub my eyes. Emery's outside pulling on his boots.

'Wait for me!' I say.

GONE TO GROUND

We stand on top of the rise, the burnt-out shell of the house in the distance smoking, just a couple of tin sheds next to it left standing.

'I can go over by myself,' Emery says, looking like he really don't wanna go near the place.

'I'm going too,' I say. 'I can handle it. You don't have to keep trying to protect me.'

Emery looks at me like he don't really believe that, but he nods, and we head on down there together, five dogs trotting along beside us.

Nothing's left of the house. It's gone to ground, black and smouldering mounds of things that I can't figure out what they used to be. I think I can pick out a toaster, definitely a stove, a fridge, but there's bits of stuff I have no clue what they once were.

Emery goes to check out the fridge, stomping over the hot charcoal, hauling at the door, but the seals are gone and it's full of black. There's nothing in there for us that's edible. 'I think they took all the cheese,' he says.

I walk around the front of the building and I see a body in a chequered shirt slumped on the driveway. It's Ted. He's got his back to me, one arm flopped out behind him. I take a few steps towards the body. I'm thinking I need to see if Ted is still alive, but I can't make my feet move that way. So here I am, maybe twenty steps from Ted and I can't make my feet take those twenty steps. I can't help him. I lean forwards so I have to step, and that gets me three or four steps closer.

Bear bounds past me, running at the body lying there, and even he stops before he gets there and sticks his nose out carefully, sniffing at Ted. He shakes his head and turns back, runs away sneezing like something got in his nostrils he didn't like.

'Ella!' Emery calls, then he's there beside me, grabbing me like he's stopping me from going any closer. 'We don't need to see dead people, Bells,' he whispers, and pulls me away.

'We should bury him or something,' I say.

'No, leave him to the foxes. If those people come back for the rest of the potatoes and fruit, they gotta see the place just like they left it. Come pick some fruit. Ted would want us to have it.'

I nod. Even though I'm swallowing down vomit crawling up my throat, I go back to the little orchard beside the burnt-down house, find a few plums and apples and apricots that are ready for eating, polish the smoke off them on my trousers. I can't get many, coz my arms are heavy like planks of wood, but I keep going and fill Ted's blue bucket halfway. We head back down past the potato crop and stop so Emery and Rooch can dig up a few potatoes for us and top up the bucket. I just stand and watch. It's like my arms have died now. They're just floppy like Ted's are, flopped and useless on the ground.

Back at the tent, I feel real tired suddenly, body tired, dead tired, and crawl onto the sleeping bag.

'We should get moving. Away from here,' I say.

Emery shakes his head. 'There's fruit and potatoes for us, and we can hunt for the dogs. We should rest here a couple of days, let the people who did that move on to a different area. Then we'll go.'

I don't say anything. I just close my eyes and think of our little flat, pretend I can hear Dad in the kitchen cooking up a batch of bickies.

'I'm gonna go along the creek, see if I can find the dogs some food,' Emery says.

'Okay,' I say, and I sniff in the smell of Dad's bickies. How long since we had flour for bickies, butter for bickies? A year, two years? I miss Dad so much. Seeing Ted lying there on the driveway to his house, like he was trying to protect it, makes me think of Dad. Where is he? What if he's lying dead somewhere too, his skinny arms flopped and useless? I can't say that to Emery though. I don't want him to think about Dad like that.

'You okay here alone? Want me to leave a dog? I won't go far,' Emery says.

'I'm okay,' I say, but I think I'm broken.

Emery goes off with the dogs. The sun warms my back, and I wrap up in my sleeping bag real tight and sleep.

GOING OUT INTO
THE WORLD AGAIN

The dogs come back panting and sweaty, feet and faces wet from the creek, blood around their muzzles and stinking of meat. They flop down all around me, and Emery comes in a little while later.

He has the knife in its leather pouch strapped to his thigh and there's blood up his arms that he's missed washing off in the creek and a wild look in his eyes. The world has turned upside down and Emery is already walking on his head.

He kicks his boots off and sits on the sleeping bag. 'Got another skin-and-bones roo and found an already dead possum,' he says, then yawns and lies back, hands behind his head. Soon him and the dogs are sleeping the hot afternoon away.

I feel silly that I see a dead person and I'm shaken to bits. I'm not walking on my head. But then I remember that's normal. That's what normal people do. Ted was nice to us. He was a nice person who thought other people were nice, like us, just passing by, and happy to take a plastic tub of cheese and go. I said Dad wouldn't want us to be worse people, but really, I'm thinking Dad just wants us to be safe and alive, even if we have to run away when good people need help.

I tell myself they would've taken Mrs Ted to look after the goats, so she is safe somewhere, and after this is over she'll come back to her farm with her goats and make cheese again and live in a brand new little cottage.

When we go back up to the farmhouse ruins later in the day, I can't go closer than the potato patch, so Emery picks fruit and I dig up potatoes, then we light a fire, and cook up all the potatoes we have in the pot, scrubbing them in the creek, throwing them in and pulling them out until we have a huge collection of potatoes cooked in their skins sitting on the backpack. Then we put the fire out right away.

'We don't want anyone to see the flames,' Emery

says, looking up at the smoke as it disappears into the clouds above us in the darkening sky, rubbing the back of his neck.

Having as much to eat as you want is amazing, but less amazing if it's potatoes. After two, I can't fit any more in. They're dry in my throat. I give each of the dogs a potato to stop them all staring at me and licking their lips. It'll fill their bellies... or gum up their throats, either way they'll stop begging. Oyster's happy to wait until it's her turn for a potato and Maroochy doesn't growl at her sitting so close. It seems like they're all learning to get along.

I have a few plums and lots of water cold from the creek to wash down the stodgy potato.

Two days later, with the sky turning pink as the sun sinks behind the bank, we have a backpack full of fruit and cold boiled potatoes, a bucket of raw potatoes, a dead roo and two possums hanging from our cart, all ready to go the next morning. Even the dogs are in their harnesses and the gang line laid out so they only need to be clipped in. They're a bit confused when we tell them it's time for sleep not running.

I'm terrified to be going out into the world again. I can't hardly believe it was me sneaking through the dark of the city just five days ago.

In the dark, I whisper to Emery, 'Maybe we should just stay here forever?'

Emery whispers back, 'We'll run out of roos for the dogs soon, and other people will be heading out of the city, find the fruit and potatoes, find us. Plus Dad and Jackie will be worried.'

'You think they're okay?' I ask.

'They're fine, Els. They'll be travelling to Ma's too by now. And we're fine and it's all gonna be okay,' Emery says.

'You can't promise that,' I whisper. 'You don't have to. I'm tough.'

'Yes you are,' Emery says.

'We'll do it together,' I say.

SILENT GIANTS

It's not even light when the zipper goes and Emery lets the dogs out. I scramble up, pull on my boots and roll the sleeping bags up tight and stow them on the cart. There's a touch of light at the edge of the sky. And somehow Emery is managing to pull down the tent in the dark.

'How will we see where to go?' I ask.

'I've had a look at the first bit yesterday, and the sky will lighten up real quick. We have to get moving because there's two towns we have to sneak past and if we can't keep below hills, we'll really stick out and have to stop somewhere till it gets dark again,' he says.

We set off and the sun does come up quickly. Emery

gives me the map, and we check it constantly as we try to stay low on the land, following the creek first, then between two hills, even though we see farmhouses on the top who could be looking down on us. There's a road ahead so we turn off and go over the hill and into another dip in the land. From the top of the hill, the dead land spreads out below us. A town sits in the distance, low houses and trees strung out along a railway line, and at one end of the town, like giant guards, stand tall pale towers, five of them. Silos, ready to load grain onto the trains. Silent, empty silos, waiting for grain that won't come and trains that don't run. They look sad, standing there so tall and proud, like they're now full to the top with the town's memories of better times.

The sun climbs higher and it's so dry here that behind us plumes of red dust are being kicked up by dog paws and tyres. We're leaving a red trail, wafting up and pointing to us like a giant red arrow in the sky.

'Emery!' I say.

'Woah!' he says, and 'Slow, Roochy, slow!', and we slow the cart right down so it's just a tiny puff of dust we're kicking up. The dogs aren't happy about not running fast. They love to run fast. We keep going till the sun's burning our heads and the stink of the dead possum is making me feel ill. There's another road ahead, so we turn away again and go looking for somewhere to hide. Eventually we find a dried-out pond between the two hills that is still damp enough to keep a couple of twisty old willow trees alive and we scoot in there under the hanging branches. I take the dogs off the gang rope and tie them to the trees, then give each of them some water while Emery carves up a possum and one of the legs of the roo.

'I think I'd like a nice piece of roasted roo,' Emery says, waving a chunk of bone with a bit of meat on under my nose.

I screw my nose up and turn away. I'm not so sure that's gonna be tasty even fried in batter. We've not had anything fried up in batter for a couple of years now. I miss it so much I probably would eat old roo battered.

The dogs eat and sleep. And we get through a couple of potatoes and some fruit, and kick back in the shade too. Sometimes the rumble of a truck or whir of a car drifts over the hill from down on the road, but it's not really busy down there.

Emery unrolls the map and follows the roads with his finger. 'We'll cross the road later in the day. We have to cross it here to sneak between the towns. After that, far less people. It's mostly country all the way up to Ma's.'

He runs his finger right up between towns and roads winding around patches of bushland and little lakes almost to the river border.

'Easy!' I say, and we both laugh coz it's not gonna be easy, and we're not even halfway yet.

GET TO THE GULLY

Late afternoon, with the sun real low, we give the dogs more water and clip their harnesses back to the cart. I ride the cart, working the brakes as Emery leads Maroochy up the hill between us and the road.

'Woah, now! Woah!' he tells all the dogs to make them quieten down. He gets them all sitting and staying and then he climbs to the top of the hill alone and looks all around.

He comes back shaking his head. 'There's still a heat haze on the road.'

'There's only been a few cars and things down there all day,' I say.

Emery nods. 'Let's just go then. There's a patch of bush and a gully the other side, we'll just go straight for that.'

'Line!' he yells, and the dogs leap up on the gang lead, pulling it straight. They start up yelping like they can't wait to be moving, as Emery takes over the handlebars from me and pushes the cart off. 'Mush! Hike! Hike!' he yells.

The dogs throw themselves into the harness, barking like wild things, like they're telling the whole world we're here, but they quieten down with the strain of heaving us two over the top of the hill, then we're off down the hill, flat out, bouncing over the rough dirt, giant trail of red dust kicking up behind us, prickles whipping at my shins.

Emery is working the brakes so the cart don't bounce into Oyster and Squid's legs, and calling, 'Haw a bit, Haw a bit!' so we're lined up towards that patch of bush and the gully, so far away it seems. He slows them down to cross the ditch beside the road, then we're up over the road and down into the ditch on the other side, and then up into the wide dirt paddock.

Three tyre tracks and dog prints for miles when I look back. Cut into that bare hillside like a blazing sign that we went this way. Cut into the land this side of the road. Hopefully when the dust settles and night falls nobody will see them, and maybe some wind will be along overnight to blow them away.

There's something moving up on the road, but I can't hear a thing. The heat haze off the black road is fuzzing up the shape, even as the sun dips down behind the hills ahead of us. It's not a car, it's too small and broken to be a car. Maybe two people walking or on bikes. But no. They're moving too fast.

'Someone's coming!' I yell.

'Hike! Hike!' Emery urges the dogs, already flat out running.

Lights come on, one light on each shape, and they're too big to be little bike lights, they're running too smooth to be torches. They must be motorbikes but still no sound. No roar, no whine...

'They're electric motorbikes!' I yell. They'll catch us on motorbikes!

We're way across the flat, crossing an old fence line at a place where it's clear of wires, though it's hard to see little wires in this light. From where the bikes are, we probably just look like a ball of dust. And it's getting darker fast. Maybe they won't bother following us.

The bikes slow and climb down off the road and start across the paddock after us. Their lights are white stripes bouncing around, lighting up the almost-dark behind us. All they have to do is follow our tyre trail. The bush and the gully are ahead, and I don't know if we'll make it to the gully before the bikes catch up.

'Hike! Hike!' Emery shouts, and the dogs are running hard. They like to run hard, they don't care why, they always give it their best, but I don't think they got enough to outrun a motorbike.

Emery is yelling at me. 'Take the handlebars. Get to the gully, unhook the dogs if you have time, if not just hide!'

'What?' I say.

'I'll catch up,' he says. 'Keep going!'

'Wait!' I yell, but he's thrown himself down into the dirt and he's rolling behind a couple of tree stumps, scrabbling around for rocks, and the cart goes on.

And I want to stop the cart. I want us all to fight those bikers together, but the dogs keep running and I steer the cart behind them, straight at that patch of bush. And a track opens up ahead of me like I wished for it, like a vehicle has been into the bush from here before, and I tell the dogs to 'Haw!' and they turn down it, and with big trees either side of me, it's almost too dark to see anything.

'Woah!' I yell, and the dogs slow, and I shove the brake on. 'Woah!'

A gunshot cracks the night. My heart leaps into my throat and I croak out a scream. Lights are waving around cutting through the dark behind me and another shot cracks off. And Maroochy is growling.

I drive the cart into the bush beside the trail, tip it over and wrap it around a tree trunk. I won't leave Emery there to die. I have to go back for him. One light is bouncing around coming for the trail behind me. I feel around for a stick or something to fight with, but all I find is that roo carcass, fallen off the cart, and that's what I grab.

I run back up the track, dragging the skinny roo with the one back leg missing, making it lighter. The dogs are all yelping and barking behind me. They wanna be helping Emery too.

The light aims square down the trail and I dive into the trees.

The dogs are lit up, bouncing and pulling on their harnesses, yelping, coz the cart's stuck on the tree, and the bike picks its way down the rough trail towards them. The light blinds me as it gets real close, and I shut my eyes so it don't ruin my night vision. Then, when the whir of the electric motor is on me, I step out, dragging the roo by the tail. I swing it up around my head once and bash the rider across the back. He crashes down and the bike slides ahead. At the edge of the light, a revolver bounces on the track. I run after it, pick it up and run around the man trying to get to his feet. I use the butt of the gun to bash the bike's headlight in. Three goes, it takes, that thing is solid! Then I bash in the red tail light and I'm blind, seeing spots, but I stumble towards the sound of dogs. I roll my ankle, crash to my knees and jump up again. I run smack into Maroochy's bouncing black fur and unclip her harness from the gang rope, and then Wolf and Bear. I leave the two white dogs stuck there, because the man on the ground is already up yelling and fighting Maroochy off, dragging his bike, trying to get it up maybe.

He flicks on the indicator lights, and in the orange flashes, he sees us, circling him, three dogs and me standing pointing his revolver.

Maroochy's got him by the leg or something. He's yelling, bashing an arm at her, and Wolf and Bear are trying to get a chunk of him too, following her lead. He better not hurt my dogs.

Then the bike crashes back down and boots thud as the man runs for it. Dogs on his heels, him whacking them away, or kicking them away. It's a mess of noise in the dark. Just dogs growling, claws scrabbling, and the white bits of Wolf and Bear's faces, teeth showing in orange flashes as they help Maroochy chase that man away.

FIND EMERY!

I chase the man back up the track too. I'm terrified, I'm mad, filthy angry at what they done. But mostly I have to get to Emery. Nothing else matters. The man's running to the path of light from a stopped bike. Stopped back up near the stumps where Emery is.

'Rooch!' I say. 'Get Emery!'

I stay out of the light. Trying to run silently. Without being seen. But the dogs cross the light every now and then.

'There's a pack of wild dogs down there!' the man we're chasing yells. 'And a kid with my gun!'

'Where?' the other man yells, and I aim for that sound.

Point my gun and pull the trigger. My heart's slamming in my chest, but the gun doesn't go off. I feel around the top of it for a switch or a lever or something. A safety catch like in the movies. By the time I find it and flick it, I don't know where the other man is no more, so I can't shoot. Not with Emery and our dogs out there somewhere.

Another shot cracks the air so loud, so close, I jump out of my skin. Dog claws go scrambling. The white face of Bear shoots past, eyes panic-wide, tongue flapping. He's getting out of here. My heart crawling for my stomach, I circle round on the bike. Skirting the pool of red brake light. There's a rifle stuck in a holder near the handlebars. I slide that out, then I smash out the white headlight, one blow this time, tuck the rifle under my arm and run.

The men swear, run to the bike. I stop running, line up the revolver, hands shaking like crazy, shoot at them, but even holding the handgun in two hands the blast makes my arms fly up in the air and the bullet too probably.

I skirt round back to where I think the stumps are, looking for Emery. There's black fur and a panting right at my hip. Rooch is here. Maroochy didn't run away, she's right here with me.

The men swear. 'Stay low. We'll come back for the other bike in the morning,' one says. The bike starts up, a quiet hum. In the red brake light, there's an arm with another handgun pointing my way and I hit the dirt, pulling Maroochy down with me. A man runs past the red light and gets on the back. Another gunshot cracks off, making me and Roochy jump.

'I'm pretty sure that kid that hit me with the rock is dead,' the man says.

My heart stops, all the air that's in me falls out, and I think I'm gonna suffocate. Emery. My Emery. My big brother. He can't be dead. He can't be. I should never have left him.

The bike takes off, dust kicking up into that red-light puddle trailing behind it, and sobs burst out of me. Emery. I don't know what to do. Me and Maroochy in the dirt in the dark, and I can't let her go, coz then I'll be alone. What if she runs away like Bear?

But Emery. He can't be dead. I don't know how to go on without him.

'Find Emery, Roochy!' I say. 'Emery.' And peel my fingers from her fur.

She's off into the dark and I'm crawling after her. Red spots in my eyes, staggering, bending down, arms out to find those stumps or Emery's body.

'Emery!' I call.

Nothing. Just the whirring of that stupid bike bumping across the paddock looking for the road, its hazard lights on now, to see in front of itself in orange flashes.

Maroochy is whining, snuffling. I head towards her. And he's there. Emery's on the ground. I wrap myself around him, pressing my ear to his chest to hear his heart. He's alive. He's breathing. I hug him. 'Emery, wake up. Tell me what to do. Tell me where you're hurt!' But Emery doesn't move, and I don't have a light. The lighter's back on the tipped-over cart. I don't know where Emery put his little torch.

I feel him all over. His head is damp on the side. I sniff my fingers. Blood. Blood from his head!

I'm crying, tears pouring down my face. I can't help it. I don't know what to do. I don't know how to help him.

'Rooch, sit!' I say and feel her parked down beside Emery's body. I press her down. 'Stay, Rooch. Stay!'

She yowls, and she's moving her head, licking his face most likely, like she can make him better.

I need to get the cart. I need the lighter to see Emery and we need to get away from here, but I can't leave Emery alone, no matter how much I need Maroochy to help me get the cart.

I head back out into the dark, heading for that flashing bike still lying down on the trail. As I run, I call to Wolf and Bear. I imagine the sun coming up and finding them dead or wounded by those shots. But there's a snuffling beside me as I head down the trail and Bear is there.

'Good Bear!' I tell him. 'Good doggo.' I keep telling him he's good. He's good for staying by me. He's good for helping me even though he's not a brave dog. He's found me again.

Oyster and Squid are making yelpy noises of welcome at us heading back down to them, and I pat them and tell them they're good too.

In the flashing orange light from the fallen-over bike, I pull the cart out from the tree, stand it back up, and shove all our gear back into it. Shove in that rifle I stole, flick the safety back on the handgun and shove that into a little pouch between the handlebars. I find the lighter in the pocket of my backpack and shine it all around on the ground quickly to make sure I've got everything. Then I use it to find the clips to clip Bear to the gang rope and lead him and the cart back up to the bike, flashing out orange warnings in the night. I pick up the dead roo and hang it back on the cart, then I feel around for the bike's

104

key and turn it off, pull out the key and throw it away into the bush.

Really dark now. The bare paddock ahead is a lighter black than the trail we're on, and with floating spots in my eyes, I walk, leading Bear by the gang rope up the trail.

'Where's Roochy?' I ask him. His nose is great, he'll find her.

I trip over a branch lying at the side of the trail. It's some kind of scrubby tree, smells fresh-broken like maybe the man we chased ran through it. I pick that up and drag it along too. I'm thinking I need to get Emery out of here, and I don't want to be leaving no trail like the one we already left on the hillside. I'm really missing grass now for a whole new reason. Grass would've hid our tracks.

Bear leads me straight to Rooch and Emery. I check Emery all over with the lighter. There's blood on his head, and his arm's bent like maybe it's broken. He's groaning now, not making any sense. I grab him under the armpits and drag and haul him across the basket of the cart, slump him in on his side so his head is on the sleeping bags, tuck his legs in and put his bent arm on top.

I shove the branch under the step and drag the end

105

up and hook it over the edge of the basket, and bungee tie it down. Then I stretch bungee cords over Emery so he's held down in position and maybe his arm won't flop off him. His knife is on the ground, so I put that in the pouch beside the handgun.

'Wolf!' I call. 'Wolfy-boy!' Nothing. I get out the lighter and do a quick walk around, thinking I'm just gonna find a mound of brown fur that used to be Wolf, and crying coz if I do, it'll break me, I can't handle that.

'Wolfy!' I howl long and loud into the night. Maroochy answers with her own howl, calling to Wolf, or calling to me to come back to Emery and help, I don't know.

FULL OF MISERY

I run back to Maroochy, clip her in at the head of the gang rope and bury my fingers in her thick fur. I rest my head on her forehead and tell her, 'We gotta get away, Rooch. Those people are coming back tomorrow looking for us. We gotta get far away.'

I guess we gotta keep going the way Emery showed me, at least as close as I can make out in the dark, and I pull the dogs around so the cart is facing the right way.

The dogs are yelping to get moving.

'Wolf!' I yell again. I don't wanna just leave without him, but I have to keep Emery and the other dogs safe. I just hope Wolf isn't injured somewhere. I hope he's not lying there watching us leave him. I cry again thinking about that.

I flick off the brake and yell, 'Mush! Hike! Hike!' and the dogs throw themselves into the night. I hope they can see better than me.

They slow to a trot straight off and we keep the dark lumps of bush against the lighter starry sky to one side. I'm pretty sure we're s'posed to follow it for a while on the map.

Emery wakes and groans and grumbles and goes quiet again. I don't think this is good for him, all this bumping, but getting found tomorrow by those guys I shot at is gonna be worse.

He wakes a little while later and he's crying and moaning, begging me to stop.

'I'm sorry!' I say. 'We gotta get away. We gotta keep moving while it's dark.' I cry along with Emery for a while, my heart breaking for him. It's not fair. He goes quiet again, and I lean down and rest my hand on his chest. Make sure he's still breathing. Why were those people so mean? Why couldn't they just let us pass by?

After a while I stop the dogs and give them some water. I hack some bits of roo off and feed them while they sit there, still harnessed to the cart.

I check Emery, he's sleeping again while the cart is still, so that's best.

We set off again, and soon we leave the bush outline behind and head out across harder ground. I'm glad coz it means the tyres won't leave such deep tracks. The stars are the only things left to guide me now, and I try to keep a really bright group to one side. I panic that they're moving and they'll send me in circles. I dunno what stars do as the planet turns. I'm sure they move in the sky or something, but which way? After a couple of hours, clouds drift over and they're gone anyway.

Maroochy runs into a wire fence and all the dogs bunch up. I haul at the brake on the cart just before it bangs into them all and get out my lighter and check it out. The wires are snapped and curling everywhere, and I have to untangle Maroochy and lead her out. Then I turn the cart around so I can lead her along the fence line until we find a gate, my legs so tired, like I done all the running, and set off again overland. There's a few trees, but the land seems to still be really flat, so we keep going through the dark.

The dogs are panting, heads down. The cart is heavier without big Wolf to help pull, but the other dogs are still trotting on, doing their best.

Clouds drift across the stars and the smell of wet dirt hits my nose. Then it rains, and I worry that it's gonna wash our smell from the ground, and Wolf, if he's out there, will never find us, but then the rain will wash away our tracks as well and right now we need that so bad.

'Woah!' I yell, then get off and get the dogs to just walk beside me for a while. They've run too long without a rest. All through the night almost, when normally we don't run them more than two hours without a rest, but we can't stop until we find somewhere safe.

The rain is cold and I'm shivering, even if the dogs can't feel it through their warm coats. Emery starts moaning again.

'Ella!' he cries.

I stop Maroochy for another rest. Tell them all to sit. I haven't got any more water for them.

'Are you okay, Emery?' I ask.

'No,' he moans.

'We have to keep moving. Another hour maybe,' I say. The sky is a little lighter. It won't be long before I can find us somewhere to set up the tent and give everyone a rest.

Emery is shivering just like me, and I pull my hoodie out of my backpack and tuck it around him.

Then I go and get the dogs back up and walking. I put my head down against the rain and just put one foot in front of the other.

I'm so wet it doesn't matter if I cry or my nose runs. I can't tell what I'm doing, just hauling in deep sobbing breaths, my throat aching, and putting one foot in front of the other, one hand buried deep in Maroochy's warm neck fur.

Me and Maroochy, dog-tired and full of misery, just trying to get Emery somewhere safe.

UNDER THE BRACKEN

The sun peeks over the horizon, the sky fills with light, and I head for a dark gash in the land. It must be a creek.

There are two farmhouses off to one side but they're sitting quiet. No lights on. No dogs barking. Maybe they're abandoned. So many farmers headed for the cities when the grass first died, looking for food the government was handing out.

The government was still promising to hand food out to people, even after they stopped. Lies, Dad said. To stop people panicking. I wonder if the farmers are heading back now. Or maybe other people left the city looking for empty houses, and they found these and are hiding in them.

The dark gash through the landscape is a really deep gorge. There's a tiny track leading down into it, so I hop back onto the cart and tell Maroochy to take us down there, working the brake and the handlebars to keep the cart on the trail as it winds down between spiny bushes and under low-hanging trees.

This is looking good for hiding. We're so wet already it doesn't really matter when we hit the creek.

'Gee!' I call, and Maroochy turns, and we bump along the edge in the shallows. Poor Oyster and Squid are having to drag and strain to get the wheels over the creek rocks and through the mud, me off and walking alongside the cart coz it's already heavy enough with Emery in it, but finally I find a bit flat enough and well-hidden enough to pitch a tent. I get the cart up there and stop the dogs, then let them off. First thing I do is pull off the roo and hack it into four pieces. First piece for Rooch, just like Emery does.

Then I move the tent out gently from under Emery, who's lying there, breathing through his teeth, eyes squeezed shut, like he can't stand to see this world no more.

I set up the tent just as the first bit of sun slides over the top of the little gorge. I push the tent pegs into the soft sand and get the two sleeping bags in there, rolled out. They're only a little wet in patches. But I don't think I can move Emery with his arm bent like that. I hunt around the creek until I find a big hunk of bark, a little curved on the inside.

Emery screams when I lift his arm and slide it under, and I start to cry again coz I don't know what to do. Emery isn't telling me, coz he's in too much pain and I don't know how to fix it. I fold up two T-shirts and put them either side of the lump on his arm, and then I take the bungee that was holding him on the cart and wrap it around and around and around, above and below that ugly swollen lump on his arm.

'Emery,' I say, 'move to the tent. You can lie down properly there, get some sleep.'

I hold his arm in its bark shield and haul at his other arm with my other hand until he's out of the cart, onto his knees.

'Come on,' I say. 'Get in the dry.'

He takes his wrapped arm and holds it against his chest, then I help lift him to his feet and into the tent.

I go fill the drink bottle and get him to have some

water. Then I'm back out into the rain, pulling branches up from the creek, and cutting bracken stalks, trying to hide the tent and cart. I unload the rest of our gear, including the two guns, into the tent. Then me and four tired, wet dogs climb into the other side of the tent and I zip it closed. I'm soaked, we all stink, but the sun climbs high in the sky and we are warm in here at least, so we all sleep. Me, I've got that handgun right beside me, but there's no way I can stay awake to guard. I just have to rely on Maroochy's good ears.

Later, when I wake up, my legs ache, my arms ache, but I suppose it's nothing compared to Emery. There's blood all up the scalp on one side of his head, but it just looks like a gouge there, on through his scalp, a bloody line, with all the hair gone, and that bump on his arm is turning blue-green.

I give the dogs each a cooked potato and eat one myself, and then a pile of plums and I feel better.

Emery wakes with a start and says, 'Ella! We have to get away!'

'We did,' I say. 'We're safe now.' But I don't know how long for. It's whether those guys are chasing us or not.

'The dogs! They'll shoot the dogs!' he says.

'They're here. They're safe,' I say, and he won't be

115

able to see the difference between four dogs crammed into a small tent and five. It's just a mass of hairy bodies everywhere.

'But they'll find us!' Emery says, and groans, reaching for his head, but then grabbing his other arm like he's not sure which bit hurts more.

'It's the middle of the day and we're hiding in a gorge, under a pile of bracken. And I have a gun,' I say. He looks at me like maybe I've really lost it, and goes back to sleep.

I want to wash and cover that bad cut through his scalp. It bled a lot last night, I think. It's still bloody now and it's all through his hair and on the bottom of the tent. But I don't want to wake him again.

SLEEP LIKE WILD DOGS

I'm trying to decide if there's any point to us moving from here right away. Emery's still hurting, so we won't be able to move fast, and the rain maybe covered our trail in, but it might not be raining late in the afternoon, and we'll probably only end up somewhere worse for being found. I guess we're all too tired and just have to hope this is a good hiding place.

The rain stops and I take the dogs down to the creek for water, then tie them to the trees next to the tent so they can't wander. And while they sit in the sun, I cut up our last possum. Already missing a few bits. I guess I couldn't expect Oyster and Squid not to have had a go at it when I left them alone.I feed the dogs half the possum and cut the other half into five chunks I put up in a tree. It's starting to stink but I figure the dogs can have it for breakfast tomorrow. They don't mind a bit of stink.

I leave the dogs eating and take a walk around, head back up the trail. See if I can see anyone moving about up above on the flats. See if I can see Wolf looking for us. It seems really quiet, but then those guys had electric bikes so that means nothing. There's no trail from us heading in last night. So that's good.

I head back to the tent. I pick a few blackberries, growing in the sun beside the track. What I notice is there's lots of blackberries down low, but hardly any up high. Is it birds or people or roos eating only the top ones and leaving the bottom?

It makes me find more bracken on the way and pile it up around the tent and over the cart. I don't want anyone seeing it from anywhere and coming down for a look-see.

Emery stirs and sits up. 'I gotta pee!' he says, holding his good hand out of the tent. I pull him to his feet and help him walk, but he pushes me off. 'I'm fine,' he mumbles and stumbles off to some bushes.

The dogs are all standing up, panting happy and bouncing to see their Emery back on his feet, and the moment I been dreading is here. Emery turns, holding his arm to his chest, and looks at the dogs, and he's still looking. He's looking for Wolf. His eyes are all scrunched up like the sunlight is too much for them, like he don't believe what he's looking at.

I swallow. My heart sinking. It's bad enough I've been worried about Wolf. Worried about leaving him behind, but now I have to explain it to Emery.

'Was Wolf shot?' Emery says.

'I don't know. It was so dark.' My voice rushes out like I'm making excuses. And I am. I didn't know what to do. I didn't know what the right thing was. Did I do the wrong thing? 'I thought I saw him running away with Bear when the gun went off, but only Bear came back.'

'Did you look for him?' Emery asks, like he forgot it was dark and he was just shot and I was panicking.

'I looked but it was too dark. I called him. He would've heard us leaving. He'd know which way we went. I just don't know why he didn't follow us.' I slap at the tears on my face.

Emery takes a deep breath, squeezes his eyes shut. 'It's okay. You did good. But they might come back and find us. We should get further away.'

I smile. 'We did. We're not in that patch of bush.

119

We're in a gorge way across the flats.'

'You got us that far away?' Emery asks, looking round like he's someplace new.

I nod. 'And look!' I lean into the tent and lift the sleeping bag to show the rifle and the handgun.

'What?' he says, his mouth drops open. 'But they're definitely gonna be coming for us now. Guns are gold.'

'But I had to take them,' I say. 'They only left coz they thought I was gonna shoot them.'

Emery says a little 'Ha!' then squeezes his eyes shut and groans. 'I wish I could've seen it. I wanna go looking for Wolf, but my head hurts so bad. And my arm.'

'It's quiet here. I think we can stay till you're feeling better. I checked around for Wolf before,' I say. 'We'll look again later.'

I help Emery back into the tent and give him the water bottle and some potatoes and fruit. He picks at it, rubbing his forehead, scrunching his eyes. I unfold the map and try to figure out where we are. Emery squints at it and I point to a gorge with two houses above it. We're still on course for staying away from towns.

Emery pushes out a smile. 'Did good, Els. Did good,' he says and lies down again.

I feel better except about not being able to find Wolf.

He prods at his scalp. Checks his fingers. 'What's it look like?'

'Looks like someone took a knife and carved a strip off your head,' I say. I pull my last clean T-shirt out of my pack. It's a long-sleeve one so it works great to fold and tie around Emery's head and cover up the bullet gouge.

The sun goes down, I bring the dogs in and we all sleep.

In the night, I dream we're back in the city and the sirens are going and people are smashing up a building, and it's making our flat shake.

'Ella!' Emery's shaking me.

Bear and Maroochy are howling. Howling so loud.

'Shh!' I say and pull on their collars.

We all listen. Somewhere out in the dark is another dog howling.

Rooch is nudging the zipper.

'It's Wolf!' Emery says.

I pull the zip up.

'What are you doing?' Emery says.

'Going to get him,' I say.

'No! Those men might have him. It might be a trap.'

I fumble around for the handgun. 'Then I'll get him back,' I say, coz family is family, even a big old doggo.

I let Maroochy out, tell Bear and the others, 'Sit. Stay!' and zip up the tent.

'Wait!' Emery is saying. But I don't wait.

By the time I turn around, Rooch is gone. The black dog gone into the black night, and it's just me trying to use my memory to remember the way to the trail. I stumble on creek rocks, trying not to fall or get turned around. There's a howl again, far away and Bear answers it behind me. That sets Oyster and Squid off, and Emery hushing them all.

There's an excited yowl further up the trail. Rooch is keen to run and find her friend Wolf, and I hope she brings him back real quick, before I get completely lost.

The bare land is a little lighter than the trail when I finally make it, staggering up to the top of the flat. There's a half-moon and a sky full of stars giving off a touch of light. I stick to the edge of the bush around the gully. I don't want no one seeing me if they're up here. No sign of Roochy. No lights. No noise. Then a yip in the darkness far away. And an answering yip, like two dogs meeting each other again. I give them a little while, keep listening. The dog noises are nice happy snuffling and little yowls and those goofy malamute talking noises. They're such silly doggos when they're happy. It all seems okay.

122

'Roochy!' I call softly. Then a bit louder. Then I wait.

The panting noise reaches me first then the scrape of paws on dirt, then a black smudge bowls out of the night and into my legs. Another with a pale bit of face and pale legs circles me.

'Wolf!' I call. 'Come here, Wolfy!' but he's not doing that. He keeps circling me, like he don't trust me no more. I get down low and hold out my hand and he sniffs it and then ducks away when I reach for him. Poor scaredy Wolf.

'Come on, Rooch,' I whisper, 'let's get back to Emery.' Maybe Wolf will let Emery check him out.

But Wolf doesn't. He slinks to the tent to nuzzle at Bear through the side of the tent, and then when I get there, he darts away again.

'Is it Wolf?' Emery asks and unzips the tent.

'Yep, but he's acting like we hurt him or something,' I say. I put Rooch back in the tent with Emery and he tells all the dogs to sit.

'Wolf! Come on, Wolf!' Emery says but Wolf is staying just far enough away. I reach into the tent and get a couple of cold boiled potatoes out and then haul down two of the smelly chunks of possum meat I was saving for tomorrow. I guess I'll just have to cut the rest of the lumps smaller. I hold them out for Wolf, but he won't take them from me. I put them on the ground, and back away to the tent.

'Poor Wolfy,' I say.

'Maybe he'll want to come in later,' Emery says and rubs his head. 'At least he's alive and not lost anymore.'

Emery goes back to sleep and I lie awake in the dark listening to Wolf scuffling outside the tent, probably making himself a little scratched-out hole to sleep in, like wild dogs do.

POOR WOLFY

I get up as soon as the sky gets a little light coz I haven't been sleeping. I been trying to figure out what's wrong with Wolfy. I open the tent quietly, telling the dogs to sit, but that's not gonna work, they all want to be out. So I stick my head out and look around, make sure there's no sign of anyone, and then open the tent fully, and let the dogs out.

Wolf leaps up from beside a tree to say hi to them all, and the first thing I see is that his ear's been shot right off. Just a ragged bloody stub of ear is left. Then something round and white flashes against Wolf's brown fur. It's clipped to his harness. I throw myself into the dogs and grab his harness, twist and pull the tag off, then let him go before he drags me over.

It's got a wireless symbol on it. A tracker!

'Wake up! We have to get moving!' I yell at Emery.

Emery's up on his knees, arm held to his chest, looking around to see what the problem is.

I hold up the tracker. 'They caught Wolf and put a tracker on him. I'm gonna run it somewhere far away to give us some time. Keep the dogs here till I get back.'

'Ella! No! They'll track you!' Emery says.

'I got to, or they'll wake up and start tracking it to right here!' I run. Emery's behind me, calling the dogs back. I scramble across the creek and into the bush. Sticks and bracken scratch at my arms as I scramble up the other side of the little gorge. I scramble right into a pile of blackberry canes and stop and pick myself back out carefully, unsnagging my T-shirt. Then I run along the top of the gorge. I figure if they have to cross the gorge to get to the tracker, it might slow them down. A farmhouse is up here, and I head towards it. There's no sound coming from it, no lights are on. I think it's empty. If I throw the tracker right underneath it, maybe they'll think Wolf has gone into hiding. They won't be able to get under there to check for sure.

I stay low and run flat out for the house. There's still not enough light that anyone up on the road behind the house or anyone looking across the land can see very well, so I think I'm fine.

I push through the wires of the fence around the house and reach between the boards at the bottom of the house and fling the tracker, hard as I can, into the centre.

As I head back to the fence, I check out a shed. Its door's propped open, and there's tools and duct tape and stuff hanging on the wall. The roll of silver duct tape is huge, just the kind of thing that would help Emery's arm, stop it moving. I climb up on an old esky and pull it down off a nail. There's a styrofoam box sitting next to it. I grab that too.

I'm just squeezing back out through the fence, when a door at the house opens and a man shouts, 'Hey!'

I sprint for the line of trees in the gorge. I don't look back until I get there and get under cover.

No one's following. Just someone trying to scare me off.

I run a bit, hide, check around me, run again.

By the time I get back to Emery he's got the dogs sitting next to their harnesses, and Wolf, who's still wearing his, already clipped into the gang line. He's got the tent down and lying in a messy heap with the sleeping bags on top.

'Where have you been?' he says, face screwed up, holding his arm against his chest like he's been banging it and it's killing him.

'I bought us some time,' I say, and I hold up the tape and the box. 'And I got this stuff so we can make a cast for your arm.'

First, I pull the meat out of the tree and cut two of the hunks in half again. I give the biggest uncut hunk to Wolf for a change, since he's behind on snacks, and while they're busy chewing on that stinky old possum, I wipe the knife on my pants and go to work measuring the styrofoam box against Emery's good arm, and cutting out one half of it so it makes a cradle for his other arm, from his elbow right down to his fingers.

'So you sit your arm in here, and coz it's a corner, it's strong and straight, and I'll cut another bit for the top, and if we tape it all together, you'll be able to move around, without jolting your arm.'

I undo the bungee cord and try to hold his arm straight while I drop the bark and wrap the T-shirt around his arm to keep it soft and snug inside the styrofoam.

Emery gasps and tears fill his eyes and he's grabbing at the weight of his hand with his other hand, like it's a floppy thing, as I slide his arm gently into the styrofoam, and get him to hold that instead. Me, fighting the need to hurry, to get moving, in case those guys know where Wolf spent the night and check that out before the house, but trying so hard to be careful with Emery's broken arm. A couple of strips of styrofoam on top, either side of the lump, and then I get the tape and wind it around the whole lot, nice and tight, hand, arm, T-shirt, styrofoam, right up past his elbow even, wrapping it around his upper arm, to keep it all firm, and then I wind it back down to his hand. I don't think there's any way any part of that broken bone can move now.

Emery lifts his arm carefully, takes a deep breath and nods, then squints and grabs at his head like nodding hurts.

I hurry and roll up the sleeping bags and tent and stuff that back into its bag, stow it in the cart, and go to work on getting the other dogs into their harnesses, lifting feet and doing up clips and hooking them into the gang rope. I fill the water bottles while Emery shushes the dogs who are keen to get moving, even Wolf, who seems happier about being back with his friends. I get close enough to check his ear, and it seems to be just missing. The edge of the ear is red and bloody like something just tore it off, right across the top of the triangle. His other ear is dark fur outside, pale fur inside with a darker edge making the triangle stand out. But this damaged ear is just the bottom part of the ear and a pile of bloodied pale fur, tufting out around his pink inner ear lumps. There's nothing I can do to repair that, and I don't know if covering it will help. Poor Wolf.

THE WIDE DEAD DIRT

I have to take the handlebars because Emery can't, so he sits on the foot stand with his feet in the basket, and his arm held out by his other arm to stop the bumps from jolting his arm as much as they're jolting his body.

He's got the map by his feet in the basket and as the sun comes up he's squinting around, trying to figure out just where we are.

He groans and shoves the map at me like it's all too hard. I guess I'll have to figure it out by myself for a while longer.

I'm not much good at steering around prickles and weeds, so Emery's sometimes yelping and spitting out prickle fluff but he doesn't try to tell me what to do for a change and that's good, but I think it's mostly coz he's really hurting. Between his arm and his head, he don't seem to know which one to hold with his good hand.

There's a crack of a gun somewhere way back behind us, and I look down at Emery and he looks up at me, and there's a big frown on his face as he peers back around me at the land behind us.

I'm thinking maybe that guy in the house objects to people on motorbikes wanting to check under his house for a dog that isn't there. And maybe soon they'll figure out there's no dog, and no gun-stealing kids hiding inside.

'What if we threw the guns out?' I ask. 'Will they stop chasing us if they get the guns back?'

'Maybe,' Emery groans, and then he says, 'But what if they don't and then we don't have guns to scare them off? And what if they don't find them?'

I'm looking over my shoulder all the time. No lights, nothing moving back there. The branch is still dragging and kicking up dust, but it spreads and settles again quick enough, and it's not very light yet, so it's not as bad as it was up on that hillside in the last of the light when those bikes saw us. The trail we're making looks weird, but the ground here is harder and it's not three wheels and a pile of paws no more.

There's a house at the end of a long dirt road ahead, so I point it out to Emery.

'Any lights or anything moving there?' he asks.

'Nothing,' I say.

He shrugs. 'We got a long way to go. We can't wait to sneak past every house in the dark.'

I keep the dogs going and we pass that house, only one street block away, nothing between us, close enough for me to see all the windows are covered by boards. Then we wind away between two hills down and over a creek and up the other side, and still no movement from that house.

I take a deep breath and give up watching it.

Another wide, dead dirt plain, and a couple of houses a long way off, a few farm sheds. It's just so dry out here, maybe people have moved to places better for growing vegetables.

The dry plains go on and on, only a few old fence posts left to divide them up.

'We should be thinking about finding a place to hide for the day,' Emery groans when the sun heats up.

I've seen him trying different ways to keep his arm up so it don't bounce along with his body, and after two hours of that, he's just given up and he's holding it to his chest, his face all screwed up. He don't say a thing. He's being tough coz both of us know we gotta get away from where we were.

KNOW ALL MY PEOPLE

I find us an old empty tin barn to hide out in. Probably an old hay shed from back when grass grew here. Now just a tall shed open on two sides. Nothing left of the hay, every scrap eaten by starving roos probably.

The dogs flop, panting, into the shady dust the moment I unclip them from the gang rope. I get them water, the last of the cold boiled potatoes and a bruised apple each. It's not good dog food, but they need to eat to run and this will fill their stomachs.

Dad always said there's nothing sadder than a starving dog. He said dogs have been living with humans for sixteen thousand years. That's a whole lot of time to be relying on each other, and it's sad when a human lets a dog down.

Wolfy comes snockering around my ankles with his head down, wanting his share but still afraid. I get down and rub under his chin softly.

'Silly, Wolfy. Me and Emery would never hurt you, pup.'

Emery and I eat the plums. It's not safe to light a fire here to boil more potatoes, but there's a sheet of tin lying in the hot sun, and it burns my fingers when I touch it. I've never heard of sun-dried potato chips, but I slice up some raw potatoes and lay them out on the tin anyway, to give it a try. I warn the dogs away when they come to sniff, and they're too tired to argue, eyes looking from me to the potato slices like I might tell them to eat them any second.

'That'll never work,' Emery says.

'Gotta be better than raw,' I say.

Emery lies on the sleeping bag trying to sleep for a while, wiggling like he can't get comfortable, then he sits up and spreads out the map. Squinting at it hard like his eyes hurt.

'I thought it would take us four or five days,' he says. 'But we've already been travelling a week and only covered what I thought we'd cover in three days.'

I shrug. 'It's harder than it looks on the map.'

'If we can do three hours in the morning and two hours in the evening, that's five hours a day at... about fifteen kilometres an hour... so that's seventy-five kilometres a day, and we've got about two hundred kilometres left to go. So after this evening, we still have three days!' Emery groans and sinks onto the sleeping bag like the maths killed him.

I lie down beside him. 'It's okay, if it takes us even another week, as long as we get there,' I say.

'But two hundred kilometres! We've only got raw potatoes left and no meat for the dogs. Wolf got hurt, my arm is killing me, my head is killing me, I can't think straight, and we might be being followed,' he says, and a tear trickles from his eye and rolls over the side of his face and drips off his ear. 'I thought I could do it, Els. It was a stupid idea. I should've waited for Dad.'

My heart breaks for him, my big brother trying so hard to save us all, and feeling like he can't go on, but I poke him in the side for us to be normal, and I say, 'Well then, let's give up and go home.'

Emery frowns at me like I'm stupid, then he snorts. 'That's even further away than Ma's!'

'Then we'll live in this hay barn.' I wave my hand at the corner. 'The bedroom can be there. And the lounge next to it, and over here can be the kitchen.'

'You idiot,' he says.

I smile. 'We gotta go on. You got us the dog cart, you got us out of the city. We'll make it, Emery. We will.'

'I thought we'd be further by now. This land, it doesn't feel right. I don't belong here.'

'No one belongs here. It's bare.'

'Nah, not that kind of belong. There's a feeling you get when you're close to home, you know?'

Coming home from school a long time ago, on the back of Dad's electric bike, me with my legs dangling, him wobbling side to side as he pedaled to help the motor up the last little bit before we turn into our street, then both of us with hands in the air coasting the whole of our street. Dad would laugh, and it was like the air had changed, got lighter somehow, as if we were leaving the busy city behind, even though we were still deep inside it. The only home I'd ever known, full of people, and cooking, and inventions and our three big doggos, always excited to see us.

But Emery, he had two homes.

'It's like you're right where you're supposed to be,' he says.

'And that's your grandparents' place?'

Emery nods.

'Why did they send you back to the city? Back to Dad?' I ask.

'Ma said small town minds would put me in a tiny box and I'd never break out. I told her I'd only want to come back and help her run the mushroom farm, anyway, but she said they didn't need me yet. Her and Grandma could run it and look after Ba just fine until I finished school.'

'I was happy when you moved in,' I say, even though I can't remember life before Emery came to live. I think I was six. Emery was ten, and I loved him right away. He'd visited in his school holidays before that, and Dad had even taken me to see him at his grandparents' place, but I don't remember much. I just remember how happy I was to have a brother moving in for good, and then how upset I was that half of all the school holidays he'd go off to visit his mum and grandparents and I'd be alone again.

Emery manages a smile. 'I'm glad I got to be your big brother, but I was just always waiting to go home, you know? So maybe me wanting to bring you out here, maybe that was part of it? Me trying to stick the best bits of two worlds together. When Ma said I had to go stay with Dad, I thought, why should I leave? It was them

139

guys in town doing the trouble-making, not me. And Ba was teaching me stuff about the land and our people. So I asked him to tell Ma and Grandma to let me stay, but he told me to go and live with my dad until I finished high school. He said that there were lots of parts to me, and if I ignored some of them, I'd never know who I truly was. He said I had to know all my people, coz he never did. He said I already knew my Grandma's ways, her Afghani food and customs at least, and I already knew some of what he had to teach me, but I needed to know my father's ways too. Ba said he would be there when I came home. It's not easy to be someone with lots of different parts, Bell,' Emery says. 'I wanted to just be one. I wanted to be like Ba.'

I pick up Emery's good hand, turn it over in mine, the dirt's lined into the creases in his fingers, and under his nails, like it's lined into mine. We got the same kind of hands, us two. We both got long fingers and the same curve to our nails.

'I'm glad Ba sent you to us,' I say. 'I'm glad you wanted to take me to your home.'

We doze through the heat of the day. I give the dogs and Emery the rest of the water so they don't overheat, and just take a sip myself.

Then when the sun starts to go down, I test the sun-dried potato chips and they taste like horrible brown potato slices that got left out in the sun all day and dried out. But the dogs don't seem to mind them when I offer them.

I pretend they're really yummy. 'Mmm, so crunchy, they just need a bit of salt,' I say to Emery as I chew.

He tries one and almost spits it out. It hovers on the end of his tongue before he decides to swallow it. 'Tastes like cardboard!' he moans.

I'm grinning as I give the rest to the dogs and clip them back into the gang rope. They start up their bouncing and whining, even while I'm rolling the sleeping bags back up and shoving them into the net.

THE SHADOWY SHAPE
OF HER

We head out across the plain once more. A line of small hills to one side and bare empty flats to the other, ahead and behind. With no water in any of us, I'm panicking as each bit of landscape opens up ahead with no wandering line of trees showing us a creek. Soon it will be dark, and I don't know if we should stop without finding water first. They need so much, these big dogs. They're really gonna get sick without water.

We've been going maybe an hour, maybe two, when Rooch starts checking over her shoulder. I turn my head to line my ears up, stare hard into the lowering light behind us, but I don't know what she's worrying about.

142

Then something flashes.

'Someone's back there!' I say to Emery.

He leans out, checking round my legs.

'We're being followed!' he says, and he scrambles up, getting his feet on the platform, pulling himself up with one hand, checking around the landscape. 'Haw! Roochy! Haw a bit!' he yells.

Maroochy turns towards the hills.

'We're going over the hill? They'll see us!' I say.

'Look at all those rocks. They'll have trouble following, and there might be somewhere on the other side we can hide. There's nothing this side, that's for sure!'

And he's right. Flat land forever this side of the hills.

The rocks in the hills are smooth and rounded off like giant sleeping sheep on the hillside. I'm not sure they'll slow the bikes down too much, but we don't have a choice.

Halfway up, bouncing and sliding on the uneven ground, grating between the rocks, we see them. The same white electric bikes as before. And they see us, coz they turn directly towards us.

I pull the handgun out of the pouch. 'Hang on and keep the cart moving!' I yell, and jump off the back.

'Ella! No! They'll get you,' Emery says.

'Not if they're still chasing you!' I say. 'Don't stop!' And I'm doing the same thing that got Emery shot and beaten a few days ago, but I can't think what else to do. We can't outrun bikes and guns. So I huddle, one little black hoodie rock amongst a pile of grey ones, and hope they don't see me in the gloom. I click the safety switch off the handgun that I can hardly hold, and hope that there's something I can do.

The bikes get closer, and Emery's right, they're not keen to take on the rocks of the hill in the almost-dark. These aren't knobby-tyred farm bikes, these are road bikes for smooth surfaces. The two riders get as far as the first pile of rocks and stop their bikes and get off. One of them pulls out his gun and they hike up the hillside, climbing over the rocks.

They draw level to me, and against the sky, even though they've still got helmets on, one of them looks like a woman. She stops and turns back to the guy behind her. I lift my gun and hold it tight in both hands. Line it up with her chest. Gotta hold it still this time. Hard to do with my head low so I still look like just a rock.

'This is ridiculous,' she says. 'We should wait for daylight.'

My heart stops. Mum? I sit up. How can it be Mum,

144

here, chasing us? Her helmet turns my way, for just a second, and her hand shoots out behind her and pats the air. She's telling me to stay down.

The guy comes alongside her. I duck back down.

She waves her hand at the landscape away from me. 'We could waste all night stomping around out here, when there's probably a perfectly safe way over the hills further along. We just can't see it in the dark,' she says. 'We'll pick the trail up tomorrow.'

'Yeah, well, we're not gonna catch them on foot, are we?' the guy says and turns around, boots scuffing on rocks as he sets off back down the hill.

Mum turns my way again. Holds up her thumb. And it's all I can do to stop from crying out, to stop myself from running to her. I'm staring, staring, through the gloom, like I might never see her again. Like my eyes have to know the shadowy shape of her, in case she vanishes again.

There's a yip behind Mum. The rattling of the cart. Rooch! Maroochy knows it's Mum! She's heading back to get to her. Maroochy always knows. Me, silent as a rock, begging Rooch to stop, to turn back!

Then a crack tears the night open, loud enough to stop my heart again. Is the guy shooting at Rooch?

A second later, Mum grunts, topples off the rock she's standing on. I drop the gun. Like I did it. But I didn't do it. It wasn't my gun. Boots scuff as the man runs back up to the rocks next to Mum. I shove both hands over my mouth. I don't breathe. I can't breathe. Someone shot my mum!

Another crack and the man ducks, fires back uphill. Then he's turning, listening for the sound of the cart, paws on rock, as the dogs scrabble away. The cart's scraping like it's tipped over.

The man lifts his gun. He's going to shoot the dogs!

I search for my gun. Find it. Another crack rings out behind me. Emery! How is Emery even holding that rifle with one arm?

The man shoots back, scrambles down to Mum. She's not making a sound. I lift the handgun, hold it as firm as I can, aim above his head, and pull the trigger. The gun bangs, flies up in the air. Slamming my hands and the butt of the gun into the top of my head. There's no way I can even hold this handgun still with my skinny little arms. But the man runs. Bent over, he's heading back down through the rocks. He gets his bike started and speeds off down the hill into the dark. A little pool of torchlight bounces around in front of him.

'Emery!' I shout, grabbing at the ache on the top of my head. 'Stop shooting! It's Mum!' I scramble out over the rocks, not even waiting for an answer from Emery, coz I got to get to Mum.

'Mum!' I scream, and my voice is wobbly, my arms are shaking, and I dropped the stupid handgun somewhere. Why does everyone in my family have to get shot! I'm crying coz it's too dark to see properly. I'm afraid that I'll touch her and she'll be a dead mess of blood and bones. And I'll never again get to hug her.

A SMALL BOY

I find her leg. It moves. She's not dead!

'Ella!' she says, and she's scrambling right up.

'Careful!' I say, trying to grab her.

But she's trying to grab me, she rips her helmet off and hugs me so tight and my face is buried in her neck and in her sweaty-smelling hair and I don't care, coz this is Mum, and I've not seen her in eight months and twenty-four days, and I thought I'd never see her again, and here she is, wrapped around me so tight, I can't even breathe in her sweaty-smelling hair no more, and I actually want to, coz it's her, here, heart beating in her chest right alongside mine. She pulls me back and kisses me on my cheek and my forehead where it hurts from being hit by a gun butt, but I don't care, and my other cheek and right on my lips, even! And I laugh.

'They told us one of you was dead!' she gasps.

'Are you hurt?' I ask.

'No. Well, yes, I took a dive, but Emery didn't shoot me. I faked it. For the record, don't dive onto rocks. It really hurts even with a helmet on.' Then she's scrabbling around on the ground. 'Where's your gun?'

I head back up to where I was hiding. 'Emery! Come out, it's okay!' I yell, coz I still haven't seen him.

I find the gun and bring it back to Mum.

'I want to make sure he thinks I'm dead,' Mum says, and runs back to where she fake fell. 'Get down! Ricochet,' she says and ducks behind a rock.

I get down and she fires into the ground where she was lying, another crack through the night, and down on the flat the bike's torch light swerves. He's heard that.

There's a scuff. Emery's on the rock above us, outlined against the sky, the rifle hitched under his one good arm pointing down at Mum.

'Emery!' Mum calls.

And Emery bends, droops, lets out a sob. His outline shrinks back into a small boy, just like that.

He walks down off the rock.

'How are you here? Is Dad with you?' Then he gasps. 'Did I shoot him?'

Mum wraps her arms around him carefully, not squeezy like me. 'He's not here. And you're a really bad shot luckily. What have you done to your arm?'

'They did it,' I say. 'Those men on the bikes. And shot his head, grazed a chunk out.'

'Oh, I'm so sorry,' she says to Emery, and he's sucking back the tears, big sniffs. He can't answer. 'As soon as I heard they found some kids with a dog cart, I got myself put on the bike recovery trip.'

'You're with those mean people?' I ask.

'Not voluntarily,' Mum says.

'Those mean people that hurt Emery and Wolf and been hunting us down?' I say, and I hardly believe that my mum's part of that.

'Sweetie, they picked us up three days ago. Your dad and I stopped on the road to help some people with their bike. I made the mistake of telling them I knew about electric bikes and solar panels, and next thing you know we're taken back to their camp and locked in sheds. I'm fixing their bikes and panels, and your dad's saying he can fix their petrol bikes, and can we stay with them, pretending we're so grateful for them for letting us join them and looking for our moment to escape and catch up with you two.

'As soon as they said they'd seen two kids and a dog cart, we knew it was you two. And when they said one of you was dead, it was all we could do to not break down and give ourselves away. They needed me out tonight to fix that bike you broke. They didn't give me a weapon, but I would never have let that man catch you.'

'And Dad?' I ask.

'He's built himself a key and he's sneaking out. I hope he's gone before that guy gets back and tells him I'm dead,' she says, and she's staring out across the flats at that bike's tiny lights getting smaller all the time. 'Imagine that, thinking half your family is dead?'

'What if we left the guns and the bike? Would they stop chasing us?' I ask.

'I think they'll give it up now. It'll take that guy three days to get back by the time he solar charges his bike. You'll be too far away and there's too many other groups out here. They'll be busy working on keeping what they got safe.'

'Do they got a whole pile of goats?' I ask.

'What? Goats? No. Why?'

There's a whining yowl in the darkness. 'Gotta get the dogs!' I say, and scramble down, arms out in front, picking my way between the grey rocks, searching for the dogs. Mum and Emery follow.

'Roochy!' I call, and she yips and yowls like she's stuck and can't get to me.

I run down to her, her big fuzzy black outline is bouncing and pulling, she licks my face and I run my hand along her harness and unclip her from the gang rope. She's off to find Mum, but the gang rope goes straight down next, to Bear and Wolf, in a scuffling mound struggling on the ground. Bear's wrapped up in the gang rope and Wolf is a quivering pile of dog on the wrong side of him, no space between them.

'Poor Bear,' I say, and unwind the rope, unhook his collar from where it's hooked to Wolf's collar, then he struggles back to his feet, and I feel him all over, pull his harness back straight and unhook it from the guy rope. I'm guessing Wolf panicked and tried to run before the other dogs could turn around, got on the wrong side of Bear, tangled them both and they both got dragged by the other dogs, afraid of the gunshots and the sideways dragging cart. Bear trots off to see Mum, so he must be okay. Squid and Oyster are sitting up, their white coats

152

easy to see, showing me they're fine in the darkness. Waiting like good doggos.

Wolf is a tangled, shaking mess.

'Wolfy,' I say softly. 'It's okay now, little Wolfy.' Even though he's almost as big as me. I run my hands along the harness line and unhook one leg. Then I just lie beside him, my hand on his warm back, feeling his thumping heart through his backbone, and tell him he's a good boy.

Mum's laughing coz Roochy and Bear are leaping all over her. Then she comes over, shines a tiny torchlight on us.

'Is Wolf okay?' she asks.

'He's afraid of guns,' I tell her. 'His ear got shot off.'

'Poor, sweet Wolfy,' she says, but Wolf moves away when she reaches for him. 'I saw him when that guy found him and put a tracker on him. There was nothing I could do without looking suspicious, Wolfy, I'm so sorry.

'I tried to slow that guy down so many times, but I just couldn't figure out how to ditch him and catch up with you. Good move getting rid of the tracker.'

Ma's facing Emery when she says that, her voice flowing over him, like it was Emery's idea.

'I took it and threw it under that house,' I say. 'I don't think Wolf can run anymore.'

'We'll load him into the cart and get moving. We can't stay here,' Mum says.

'The dogs are exhausted,' Emery says. 'They're hungry and thirsty.'

'There's a creek ahead,' Mum says. 'We'll go there and get them sorted and rested for a few hours, but then we have to push on and get away.'

NOTHING FOR US
OUT HERE

It's great to have Mum here with a plan, with two strong arms to help me right the cart and get it turned around, find all our spilled gear, get Roochy and Bear clipped back in. To help load poor broken Wolfy into the basket and help Emery sit there with his feet either side, to hold him calm while we walk it down over the rocks.

On the flat, Mum jogs ahead with Maroochy hot on her tail while I steer the cart, extra heavy now with Emery and Wolf in it. We get nearer to the creek, just a line of dark trees against the moonlit sky, and a smell of dampness.

Mum jogs back puffing and whispers, 'Woah!' to

155

Roochy. She stops us and runs back to me. 'Do you have a knife or something? There's a roo,' she says.

I grab the knife from the pouch.

Then she lets Bear and Maroochy off and they all run ahead.

I get off and gather up the slack gang rope and tug it over my shoulder along with Oyster and Squid, dragging the cart across the hard dirt, towards the yipping of Bear and Maroochy, and Mum calling to them in the dark.

'Good doggos,' I tell Oyster and Squid and rub their chins, coz they really want to be out there chasing roos as well, and they're bouncing in their harnesses but they keep on pulling that cart with our injured pack family in it just like me.

Mum comes back, torch between her teeth, dragging a small dead roo, with Bear and Roochy nipping at its feet like it might get up and run again. It's skinny but will fill these dogs up for now. It's so good to have Mum back.

She clips Bear and Maroochy back in to the gang rope and says, 'Come on then, let's get these dogs watered and fed.' And we head down into the line of trees. My face is in the water right away along with the dogs, even with Mum saying we should boil it first.

Then I set up the tent best I can in the dark, while

Emery sits right next to Wolf, and watches the dogs drinking from the creek and coming back to hang around Mum while she cuts up the roo. Wolfy is just sitting there shaking like the world is too mean for him to ever stand up properly again. Mum with the little torch between her teeth to see what she's doing cuts the roo's throat and she's bleeding it into the pot.

'What are you going to do with the blood?' I ask.

'I'm going to pour it over the rocks where they think I was shot,' she says. 'And then they won't come looking for me ever again.'

'But what will they think when your body's not there?' I ask.

'That you took me to feed to the dogs,' she says.

'What?' I ask.

'How bad has the world got since we left the city?' Emery asks.

'Not so bad,' Mum says. 'It's just the gangs forming up, grabbing resources. Those gangs are dangerous. That gang is dangerous. All the farms close to the city have been trashed.'

'We saw one,' I say. 'With goats.'

'Oh,' Mum says, and she hugs me tight.

Mum slices some nice thin bits of roo thigh and

cooks them on a lighter flame so that me and Emery got some roo to eat too. Then shares out the rest of the roo between the dogs. Even Wolfy comes around a bit and eats a few chunks.

She sends us to bed straight away, telling us she'll wake us in two hours. Then she puts Wolf in beside us to keep him calm and safe with his little bit of stinky meat. The other dogs she ties to the trees nearby.

It all goes silent except for the sound of dogs gnawing on bones, and we sleep.

A whir of an electric bike makes me sit straight up. Maroochy lets out a little yip, not a growl, so it must be Mum coming back. The sky is light now. Dawn's not too far away.

We pull down the tent and pack it into the cart, which Mum hauled over to the other side of the creek, hook up the dogs again, even Wolfy, who seems to be a little better after his sleep.

'It'll do him good to focus on running, not worrying,' Mum says. She pops pills from a blister pack for Emery and checks the graze on his scalp with her torch. 'This is so deep!' she says, poking around at the edges of my long-sleeve T-shirt. 'I don't think I should move this bandage until I've got something to clean it with. It might have to wait until we get to Chrissy's place.' She sighs and tilts her head at Emery. 'You and Wolf ducked just enough, but you both could've ducked a little more.' She grins, but there's tears in her eyes and she looks at me and I nod, coz we're both thinking how close those bullets came to stealing our Emery and our Wolfy away forever. Mum reaches out and grabs my hand and squeezes it, blinks away a tear.

'Will Dad be okay?' I ask, coz I just want for us all to be together and safe and the world feels too dangerous for any of us to be alone.

'He will be. You know, he found me at the power station way out the other side of the city, and he convinced them to let me leave, and got us both back home to the apartment all through that crazy, falling-apart city on an electric bicycle! Then we charged it for a day and got out of the city, probably using the same bike paths you took with the dogs.'

'We left the paths early,' Emery says. 'Too dangerous.'

'Yes, you were right. We found an old petrol truck and your dad got it going, and we had the bicycle on the back recharging, when we ran into that group struggling on the side of the road with their electric motorbike.' Mum shakes her head. 'If we hadn't had the solar roll and

159

our skills with fixing things, they would've shot us too, I think.'

'So how will Dad sneak away?' I ask.

'He was grinding a key from a piece of tin right from the first day, just by looking and recreating perfectly what he saw when they locked him in the shed every day. Such a talent for creating things. He pretended he was so happy to join their group, helping with every little fix-it job, they'll be surprised to find him gone. And all their power walls disconnected, and their camp lights and alarms completely dead.'

I smile.

'Emery,' Mum says, 'I need you on the bike. The shocks are better than the cart and I don't want your brain or arm bouncing about any more than they have to. You really need a few days just keeping still to recover.'

Mum looks at me and I nod, coz I can manage all the dogs alone. Anyway, Rooch is just gonna follow Mum and Emery on the bike. It'll be easy.

That's how we set off, Mum on the bike with Emery on the back, going slowly so Roochy just gallops off after them with the other dogs following.

Mum has to go slow anyway coz she's only got a little torch for a light, coz I smashed the headlight on that bike.

None of us have slept more than an hour, but at least the dogs are fed on that old roo, that little hollow behind their ribs not as deep as yesterday, and our water bottles are full. We head off across the wide bare plain, the wind in our faces like it's warning us there's nothing for us out here, like it can turn us back.

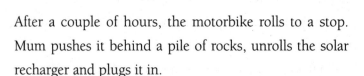

STOMACH
FULL OF GRIT

After a couple of hours, the motorbike rolls to a stop. Mum pushes it behind a pile of rocks, unrolls the solar recharger and plugs it in.

'I'll come back for it,' she says, already swiping at the dust landing on the solar roll. She helps Emery back onto the cart and gives him more headache pills.

We go on across the plains, Mum jogging alongside Maroochy, and Emery starts up groaning.

Mum yells, 'Woah!' to Maroochy, wipes the dirt from her eyes and squints around.

There's a hay barn way over on the side of the hill, and a bit of a ditch with a few scraggly ti-trees and some rocks nearby. Mum points at the scrub, coz I guess anyone following would choose the hay barn, and I yell, 'Gee, Rooch. Gee!' and turn the dogs towards it.

Mum and me get the tent set up in the bottom of the ditch and camouflaged with sticks and branches of scrubby trees by the time the sun is hot on our heads and shoulders.

Then we give the dogs water, unclip them, cover the cart with branches, and crawl into the tent. We're a mass of fur, and snores, and sweaty sleepy arms and legs and paws stretching for room and the coolness from the zipper door or tent's vents as we sleep the day away.

In the late afternoon, we wake all thirsty and our big bottles of water run out real quick.

'I'll go get some more,' Mum says.

'I'll come with you,' Emery says.

Mum shakes her head at Emery. 'You just lie still. You can't keep bouncing around with that head injury and broken arm.'

Emery opens his mouth to argue.

'No,' Mum says. 'Let me help you. Everyone needs a bit of help sometimes, Emery.'

I don't say nothing, coz this is old arguments between Emery and Mum. Her saying he needs to listen to her.

Him saying she's not his mum. But this time Emery don't push back. This time maybe he really does need her help.

I go to stand up to go with Mum, but she shakes her head at me. 'I need you to take care of Emery and keep the dogs quiet, so he can rest,' she says. 'You can't go out alone!'

'I'll take Bear,' Mum says.

And that makes me hot, like a slap to the face, because why would she take Bear and not Maroochy if she's sure she's coming back. She knows we need Maroochy to lead the cart. She knows we can get there without Bear. Which means she knows it's dangerous.

'I can do it,' I say. 'I been out there looking for water and keeping everyone safe for days.'

'I know, Baby Bell,' Mum says and pats my shoulder, like she's here to do all the hard stuff now and I can go back to being the baby of the family. It's me now feeling like Emery used to. Me feeling like I don't need help.

Mum also takes the rifle and the knife, and leaves me with the handgun. The bruise on my forehead aches from remembering the last time I used it, so I don't know what I'm s'posed to do with a weapon I can't even hold. Just makes me madder but I can't say anything. I'll burst into tears.

It takes me a while to convince Rooch that she can't go too, as Mum slips away. But eventually Rooch gives up nudging the zipper, and I can let her collar go.

'I'll take the dogs for a walk,' I say to Emery.

'Just two at a time,' Emery says. He's lying with his good arm across his eyes, elbow sticking up, like he's hurting bad.

I find leads for Maroochy and Wolf and clip them on, convince Oyster and Squid to sit so we can squeeze out without them.

Maroochy trots ahead, head up, nose to the evening breeze, tail stiff. She's looking around in the low light for anything that might get us, or maybe which way Mum went. Wolfy is slinking along hard up against my legs, head right down low, looking from side to side, licking his lips like he does when he's worried. He gets distracted for a moment by a bit of branch that needs peeing on, so we stop. Further along the ditch, Maroochy spots something and growls, sending Wolf banging back into my legs. The thing sees us too. It's some kind of rat thing, and it leaves the bottom of the ditch and scrambles away up to a hole in the bank, and the flash of a white-tipped tail is the last thing I see.

Maroochy pulls us over to where it was. Nose sniffing

and snorting like mad, she follows the trail up to the hole and sticks her whole face into it. Back where the rat thing was sitting before we scared it, the floor of the ditch is covered in scratches and they're darker than the rest of the dirt. Mud! The rat found mud. Where there's mud, there's water!

I let Maroochy go on with her snorty sniffs and drag Wolf back to the ditch. I scoop out the dirt in the bottom of the ditch and there's soft mud underneath. I get down on my hands and knees and scrape and dig like a dog. Maroochy runs down to see what I'm doing, like maybe I found another rat thing, but she licks the mud and she gets stuck in too, digging around the edges of where I'm digging.

'Good Roochy!' I tell her. Her paws are really built for digging. Humans are so useless at digging unless they've got tools. What must Rooch think of me and my stupid little claws?

This ditch must be part of a winter creek or something. Maybe there's usually water here, which is why the rat thing set up a home here, but now, with everything so dry, it's just more bare dirt and a few tufts of bulrushes, brown and dead on the outside, one or two green spikes in the middle.

Soon water is sliding down the sides of our mud hole and collecting in the bottom, and Wolf sticks his head in and laps up some water, like we're doing it all for him, and we don't mind or growl, coz he's needs a bit of looking after.

Maroochy laps at the water too, and it's just me digging and scraping till my fingernails hurt. I find a stick and use that to loosen up the mud in the bottom before I drag it out of the hole and stack it up all around. The dogs are knocking mud back in with their paws, but soon they've drunk enough, and I stack it all up on the sides again.

I get Wolf to sit beside me and Maroochy goes back to check out the rat hole, as I watch the dirt settle in the water. The sun's getting really low, dragging the heat across the land after it in a breeze, but there's enough light left that when the top looks clear, I get down on my belly and put my head into the hole. The water is gritty in my teeth and tastes like dirt, but I suppose that's not the worst thing it could taste like, and maybe the grit will fill my empty stomach and stop it from aching.

I don't even remember what it was like to feel full. Strange ideas of food pop into my head all the time, a tiny memory of taste, ice-cream and pizza, banana and mango, like my brain is trying to tell me to go get that thing, like it's forgotten that only mangoes exist now, and last time we bought one it cost forty dollars and we had to split it three ways to share, and chew the flesh off the pip like dogs gnawing on a bone. I try to fill my stomach on gritty water instead.

HOW TO SAY
WHAT I MEAN

I head back to get the pot from the tent.

'Emery! We dug a hole and found water!' I say, unzipping the tent and shoving my head in, and through the licking faces of Oyster and Squid.

'Really?' he asks.

'Really! Take Rooch and Wolf and I'll take the other dogs to get some water.' I'm so excited, I'm just bundling Wolf into Emery's arms and grabbing the pot and pulling Oyster and Squid so I can clip leads on them too.

'I wanna see,' he says, pulling Rooch in and getting up to his knees.

'You're supposed to be staying still!' I say.

'Don't you start!' he complains.

I shove the pot into his good shoulder so he sits back down. 'Stay!' I say. 'You can see it tomorrow. I'll get you some tasty dirt-water too.'

I pull the dogs out and zip the tent closed on his complaining at me, saying I'm like Mum. And I don't mind if I am like Mum.

'Oh!' Emery yells. 'If there's water, there will be bulrushes. Pull them out and bring them to me!'

'They're mostly brown,' I say.

'Just dig out the green bits then,' he says.

There are bulrushes, so I grab the green stalks way down low and rip part of the plant up, then I've got to use the pot handle to kind of dig them out. At the bottom where the stems turn to roots, there's parts that are all white. I take them back to the tent, dragging Oyster and Squid who want to be going the other way, not back where they came from, bouncing and dancing about like they haven't just spent days hauling a cart around.

'This?' I ask Emery.

'Yes!' he says, and grabs the clump and separates it up, gripping it with his knees, peels a bit out with his good hand. 'Chew on this and spit out the bits that turn to string in your mouth.' He shoves the stem of a bulrush into his mouth and chews it. 'Mmm.' Then he holds a stem out to me.

I shove it into my mouth and chew, and at first I think I'm getting nothing, but the white bit of bulrush breaks down into juice and something nutty tasting. I chew and chew as I take the dogs back to the waterhole.

I get the pot full of clear water before the dogs push more mud down into the hole again trying to get their share.

'Good little doggos,' I tell them, even though they're not little at all, they're just not huge like Rooch. 'I know it's harder for you to pull the cart than Bear and Roochy, but you're doing great.' I give each of them a big hug. Us little guys gotta stick together.

There's a 'woo-ooo' sound and Bear comes galloping out of the dark making my heart thud a couple of hard beats even though I recognised him right off.

He's panting, tongue hanging out, and happy to join Oyster and Squid head down in the hole.

Mum's following along behind, and I put down the pot, spit out the stringy bits from my bulrush meal and run to meet her.

She shakes an empty bottle when I get closer. 'Dry as a bone out there,' she says.

'No, it's not,' I say, giving her a shrug and a grin. 'I dug a hole and found water, straight away!'

'Oh, Ella! You're amazing!' Mum says. She's hanging onto something strung over her shoulder and when she slides it off, it's two goannas. 'Tastes like chicken,' she says and nudges their bodies with her toe. 'Maybe.'

I laugh and lead her to the waterhole.

She drinks half the pot and I take the rest back to Emery.

Mum digs a hole in the bank and makes a tiny fire and puts the legs and chopped-up bits of tail in there and covers the fire up with branches and her old T-shirt. The rest of the goannas goes straight to the dogs.

They're definitely happier and fuller by the time me and Mum and Emery are sitting in a huddle in the dark, gnawing on bits of bone and meat. My tongue hunting out the meat in the knobbly tail bones, my teeth nibbling off every little loose bit, then I show Mum the bulrushes Emery said we should eat.

Mum's finished and sucking meat from her teeth. 'Maybe we should stay here for another day and wait for your dad to catch up. I don't know how far away the next bit of water is.'

The way she says it, I can tell she's worried for him.

'What was the plan again?' I ask.

'He was going to sneak out after I was away. I don't think he could have made off with a vehicle, but still, even walking, he can't be far away now.'

'What if he goes right on by us in the dark?' I ask.

'It could happen,' Mum says.

'Nah,' Emery says. 'Rooch would know. Rooch always knows.'

'He's right,' I say. 'She knows.'

'If the bike is charged by now, you should maybe go look for him,' Emery says.

'No!' I say. It was bad enough when she was out there looking for water nearby. And I feel bad right away, coz now I'm saying, no, don't go rescue Dad who's out there all alone.

Emery frowns at me, but it's not his mum, it's mine, and I've only just got her back after so long.

'I mean,' I say, trying to think how to say what I really mean. 'We're safe here, and we've got water, and Emery needs to rest, so if you need to go, just for a day to look for Dad, that'd be okay. But I think we should stay together.'

GOTTA GET
TO CHRISTMAS'S

As first light edges over the land, Mum checks both the guns and stows the rifle back into the cart.

'You've got two shots left,' she says. 'There's three in the handgun, so I'll take that.'

I nod and blink away a tear, and a lump grows in my throat. I swallow that lump and I swallow the idea that Mum was gonna stay. Maybe I'm being a baby wanting her. I just gotta get back to doing what I been doing a while longer, caring for Emery and the dogs.

Mum sees the tear. 'Bell, oh, Bella. You've done such an amazing job of keeping everyone safe and finding water, and we're almost there now. We're almost all together and safe, and I know you're just worried for me and for Dad.'

I nod. 'We're a family,' I say, 'and we all gotta help each other. You go get Dad. I'll keep on looking after Emery and the dogs.'

Mum hugs me for a long time. Maybe she's considering not going. 'I wouldn't go if I thought there was any chance someone would find you here,' she says, like that's what I'm worried about. I'm not. I'm worried about losing her! 'If I'm not back in a couple of days, don't let anyone get in your way. You and Emery gotta get to Christmas's, no matter what happens. Just keep getting up and going on. We'll catch up. Promise me!'

The way she says it, it makes me think there's more trouble for us ahead, and I don't want to stop hugging her. 'I promise,' I say.

Mum hugs Emery and makes him promise too, then she waves and turns away. After eight months and twenty-four days apart, and two days together, we are apart again.

'Find us!' I shout at her jogging back. 'Find Dad and find us again! I love you!'

'It'll be okay, Ella,' Emery says. 'It'll all work out. Jacks is real smart.'

And it's nice to hear Emery call her Jacks.

He used to say he don't need another mother. Dad was always having to say, 'Do what you're told,' to him whenever Mum asked him to do something, coz Emery was angry, I guess, that he got sent back to the city to live.

Now though, with my mum the only one who can get Dad, and all of us split up, Emery's worried just as bad about his mum and grandparents. I guess we're all gonna just be happy to be safe and together no matter whose mum is whose.

WHO'S THE HERO

Emery rests and I do too for a while, then I walk the dogs, telling Emery I'm taking them to get water but really, I'm checking the horizon in case Mum is on her way back with Dad, or in case anyone else is out there. The land is as dry and red and lonely as Mars.

The wind starts up late in the afternoon, and dust swirls and sticks to my skin and makes my hair thick and even dirtier. I can't even remember what clean feels like no more.

Me and the dogs spend a while trying to dig that rat out of the bank for dinner, but it's too hard and we just wind up even dirtier, and finally I decide the rat thing is a better digger and deserves to live quietly and not be hunted down by a pack of dogs. I name him Ratty White-Tail and wish him good luck. I bet he's glad we dug him a waterhole. He's probably so glad that he's sneaking out when we're sleeping, having a fine old time swimming about in our drinking water.

The sky gets as red as the land as the sun goes down, and giant black clouds whip up into dark foamy peaks and tear across the sky, none slowing down enough to drip a single drop of water.

The wind billows and flaps the tent in the night, waking me up all the time, making Maroochy sit up and look around, making the other dogs wake up and move. So I give up on sleeping and just lie and listen to the wind, hoping to hear the hum of an electric bike.

The sun rises and the wind just keeps on going, getting hotter and drier as the sun gets higher. It's hard to get clean water from the hole. There's nothing to eat except the brown bits of bulrush and they're not tasty. It's too hot and dusty, and dirt stings my eyes whenever I leave the tent to check the horizon.

'Waiting is the worst!' I groan to Emery, and flop down beside him in the tent. All of us zipped in here to keep out of the dust, too hot, too hungry, and too grumpy.

'Maybe she's picking up pizzas?' Emery says, making me laugh.

'You're so stupid,' I say and elbow his good arm. 'Tell me a story of what it's like living at Christmas's place with your grandparents?' I ask.

'Well, Ma, she's real bossy, and her and Grandma are always up and off to the shed or the caves to look after the mushies or deliver the mushies, so she leaves lists of jobs to do, and if you don't do them you're in real trouble.'

'Really? What kinds of jobs?' I ask.

'Just dumb things, like the dishes, and hanging up washing, and making sure I get to the school bus on time. But the thing is, they're up at the caves or out all day, so they don't know what me and Ba was up to.'

'What was you up to?'

'Ba was relearning the old ways of growing and storing grain.'

I laugh coz it's not the answer I thought I was gonna get. 'What do you mean "relearning"?'

'Ba grew up in Sydney. Far away from country and his family. And he was a welder. He was no farmer. He didn't know nothing about land. But when he married Grandma she'd been working and saving for a house, so they had some money, and Ba convinced her to buy this land coz it was home. And coz of the old gold mine. He thought they'd strike gold. Grandma says they did, once she started to use the tunnel for growing gourmet mushrooms.'

I laugh. 'She's smart.'

Emery smiles. 'Yeah, her great-great-grandfather was one of the first foreign people to come to Australia. He was a camel herder from Afghanistan. She says she's got the blood of a camel trader in her veins. If you lie to her, she says she can smell it. She points at you right in the nose and says you smell like camel dung. Don't lie to her, Baby Bell, if you know what's good for you.'

'No way!' I promise. Already I'm terrified of his gran.

'Anyway, Ba said that all this land used to be full of fields of grains way back before any foreigners came to Australia. He says our people used to harvest it with long blades of sharpened stone and grind it into bread, even before the Egyptians. So he travelled around until he found some of the old grains and talked to people about the ways to store it, and he's been saving it and growing it ever since.'

'Really?' I ask. 'Will he still have it? Or will it be all dead from red fungus too?'

'I don't know. We experimented making these clay store mounds like the old ways until we got it right and that last summer, before the grass died, before the city shut down. Even though Ba was sick, we got a whole pile stored. I don't know if he kept going.'

'Maybe it was safe in the mounds you made.

Maybe it's still there?' And I'm secretly hoping that means there's warm, fresh bread waiting for us at Christmas's. I can't even remember what bread tastes like no more but that don't stop my tongue from licking my lips and my stomach from growling for it.

'I made one into an anthill shape for a joke, and Ba made me make them all into anthills. He said he didn't want people stealing them, and who'd be stupid enough to steal an anthill?'

'So what if he didn't tell anybody? They could still be there, sitting round, people thinking they really are just anthills!' I shout because the wind is so loud now. Roaring and slapping at the tent.

'This is why we should've come up here ages ago. We should've come straight up soon as the grass died, before the city got locked down and then ran out of food,' Emery says.

I'm thinking if we did, maybe Emery wouldn't be

hurt, and we wouldn't have to ride the dog cart for weeks, all of us so starving, but we would've still had to leave Mum behind.

'You're right,' I say. 'We didn't know Mum wouldn't come back in time.' I burst into tears. I'm thinking of all the things that happened to us, and how angry Emery was back home when we were waiting so long for Mum, and how close his grandparents' place is now, and him not knowing how they're going all this time, and it's all too much. 'You were so mad!' I say. 'I heard you telling Dad we had to go. But he couldn't. I couldn't. Coz Mum.'

'Shh, Bell.' Emery rubs my back. 'We're a family. We shouldn't be leaving anyone behind. I'm sorry I said it.'

I sniff. 'Really?'

'Yep.' He smiles. 'Now I'm only mad that I got hurt and you gotta take care of me, and your mum's gotta rescue Dad. I wanna be the hero.'

HEADING INTO
THE RED DUST

I dry my eyes and put my head on Emery's chest, listen to his heart thud, don-dom, don-dum, hard to hear over the whacking and flapping of the tent walls. 'You already did lots of hero stuff, you need to learn to share.' There's a wild howl of wind, high up above us. The dogs all sit up. I sit up too. All of us looking up at the tent roof, listening to the wind. I wanna open the door and look outside, but this noise, this whining from the sky, it's terrifying. It's like the sky is trying to suck us up.

I grab the loop at the centre of the tent roof and pull it down. Even though the dogs are yipping and yowling and complaining like mad, howling back at that sky,

I pull that tent roof low, squashing the dogs to their bellies. The loop jumps and burns at my fingers, the wind trying to lift up the tent. The branches we stacked around the tent scrape and bump, like the wind is tearing them off. Emery reaches up his good arm and grabs the loop too, as the wind gets up to roaring like an angry monster, and dogs go squirming and panicking over us, toenails scratching, looking for somewhere to run. Dust streams in through the vents. We cough and squint, blinking dust, and so do the dogs, coughing and yipping and squirming to run away.

'Sit! Drop!' Emery yells in his loud mean voice, and five dogs get lower. Wolf presses his head under Maroochy's belly, like he can burrow to safety under her.

The wind is so strong, our tent is a kite, and all that's keeping us from sailing away is a few tent pegs and the weight of us and five big dogs. None of us heavy enough, it seems. We're all too skinny.

The loop in my and Emery's hands leaps and jerks and finally tears from the tent. The tent bends sideways, the pole bent over our heads, banging hard against my shoulder, hurting. Then it snaps, and the ends go bouncing and smacking at our heads. We get down, me with my arms out, over the dogs, trying to keep them

184

still, hoping they don't get even more spooked by being slapped by those tent sticks. The branches outside the tent crack and slide over us, scraping my back, and fly off.

'Are you okay?' I yell at Emery, who's curled around Maroochy's head, him maybe thinking that if she's calm, all the other dogs will be as well.

'Yeah!' he yells.

We crouch that way for ages. Just hanging on. Me, wondering why the wind has turned on us as well. My back gets heavy. The tent sucks in on us. Dirt lands on the tent, squashing it, making it flat, reclaiming its land, and the wind lets up a bit.

'It's okay,' I yell, breathe, cough. 'It's okay.'

I sit up, but a massive roar crashes down on us and I'm pushed back over the dogs. The tent rips! My hair flies up, and I'm clinging to Wolf with one arm and Emery's legs with the other, my eyes shut against the dust, my face buried in Wolfy's fur. A sleeping bag slides out from under my legs and it's off into the wilds. The dust stings and burns at my neck and hands and I can't feel the other dogs anywhere, it's like they've been blown away, but I can't let go of Wolf or Emery, to find them, or open my eyes with raggedy bits of tent whipping at my head, dirt rasping at my face. And then the wind drops, slams at me a few times, then gives up.

The howling moves away across the country. Dirt falls, pattering on my back like a soft rain. And we are left alive once more.

I let go of Emery's legs and wipe my eyes. Dirt falls from my hair. Emery is okay, sitting up. Wolfy sneezes beside me. Stands up and shakes, adding another cloud of dust to the haze. The other dogs come running back to see if we're okay.

We crawl from the ripped and broken tent. The dogs gallop around, getting rid of their fear by sniffing everything to see it's safe, and sneezing coz there's still too much dust and wind. I slap the dirt off my clothes, cough some more, help Emery stand up. We look around. Dust hangs like a fog across the land.

'We'll go,' Emery says, hauling the dog cart back upright with his good hand from where it's tipped over, wedged against a scrubby tree.

'What?' I ask.

'I was going to say tonight we should go, but look how we can't see into the distance, we'll go now, no one will see us.'

'But Mum said tomorrow!'

186

'We're out of food, we've lost our water bottles and our tent. We should move while we can.'

I look around. All that's left on the floor of the torn tent is Emery's sleeping bag, the rifle, and the pile of harnesses, where he was lying. Emery saved them. I didn't save a thing, not my hoodie, not my sleeping bag, not even the pot or water bottles.

I move off in the direction of the wind thinking I can find the water bottles, maybe, the pot, my sleeping bag… but everything is a haze of red dirt.

'We can spend time setting up camp again, or we can move, Ella,' Emery says from behind me. Then, 'What do you think?' Like he meant it to be a question not an order.

I wonder how long we can last, the seven of us, sitting here, waiting for Mum and Dad, with no food and no shelter. I nod. 'I'll scrape out the hole so we can have a drink first,' I say, and stumble off towards the bank.

It's hard to see where the hole was, and when Maroochy comes, I scrape at the ground and ask her to sniff, and finally she picks a place and starts digging, and it's our hole, just collapsed in a bit, with dirt blown over it.

We all get a drink, me and Emery down on our bellies, lifting the water to our mouths with one hand. It's like I can't drink enough for what's ahead. I shove a bit of tent pole into the hole, right in the middle, so that if Mum does come back this way, she'll find it.

Then I harness up the dogs and clip them into the gang rope. Roll up the sleeping bag and stow it in the basket, along with the rifle. The pouch on the handlebars still holds the knife and the lighter and a few other things, but we haven't got much left...and our map is gone.

'How will we stay on course?' I ask.

Emery squints at the dust ahead. 'I think I'll know from here.'

So when he's sitting with his feet in the basket, I push the cart out and yell, 'Line out!' then 'Hike! Hike! Mush!' and the dogs throw themselves forwards, feet scrabbling at the dirt until the cart gets moving. And here we are once again. Two kids and five big dogs, heading into the red dust, hoping it all works out. It's just gotta work out.

WE'VE ALL GONE WILD

By the time the sun dips low, Emery's face is screwed up in pain, but he sits with his feet in the basket, squinting at the surrounding countryside, and asking me do I see a dirt road over that way, or a line of trees might be a creek that way. And when I answer, he says, 'Gee a bit, Roochy, gee a bit!' like it means something. He's saying it through his teeth like his whole jaw is locked tight.

Finally he starts crying. 'I can't handle this bumping. Find me a shed or something. Get Dad to come back for me.'

'Woah! Woah!' I say to the dogs, and I get the cart stopped. Right there in the open.

'I'm not leaving you, Emery,' I say. 'And anyway, you're the only one who knows the way to the mushroom caves. We're gonna keep going like Mum said.'

Emery crawls from the cart and lies groaning in the dust. I get the dogs to all have a sit-down too, they shouldn't be running in the afternoon. They're not built for heat.

'Come on, Emery. Just a while longer, then you can sleep. We'll do it bit by bit.' I help him sit up. He hauls himself back into the cart.

'Mush, doggos! Hike! Hike!' I yell, and the dogs take off again. Trotting along real slow, tongues out and flapping, like they could go forever at this pace. Wolf though, he's tired. Instead of throwing himself into the harness, he's running along with his head down and almost tucked under Bear's chest, like he needs to feel safe. I don't mind that he's not pulling, if he can just keep running and not ride on the cart making it heavier for the other dogs, that's enough. And if Emery can just keep telling me where to go, that's enough too. We're all doing the best we can.

Dust gets whipped up in my face, and Emery keeps coughing until he stands up. The wind gets worse. Giant whirlwinds sail across the bare dirt and all the dogs are trotting with their heads down, sneezing now and then. I'm worried another windstorm will hit, but at least this wind will hide our tracks from anyone bad out here.

We keep going, down into ditches and up the other side, past sheds and farm buildings, me blinking the grit from my eyes, watching for any movement. The dust we're kicking up swirls away to join the rest of the dust blowing around.

We pull into one farm that looks really deserted, and I try the taps near the sheds, but the pipes are dry. So we rest in the shade for a while and carry on. I'm thinking one of the dogs is going to collapse from dehydration for sure.

Emery's back sitting with his feet in the basket, a bit floppy-headed, not giving any more directions, and the dogs' toes are scraping in the dirt when I see a dam. There's a twisty old willow tree, a nice high bank on one side, a pile of bulrushes and wild brown grass around the edge. The first actual grass we've seen in forever.

'Haw!' I say and turn the dogs towards it. I stop them under the tree and get off. There's movement in the grass and I grab the knife and a stick from beside the tree and run over there. A snake! A big snake and it's not very happy to see me. It lunges at me as I leap back. I've got

191

the knife in one hand and the stick in the other, and I'm not sure what to do. This snake could feed the dogs.

Maroochy is barking behind me and Emery is shushing her and holding her back, and calling me back, telling me to get away, but I gotta kill the snake in case Maroochy gets to it and gets bitten. I'm no hunter. I don't ever want to kill anything, but this snake's not going to slither off into the dusty nothing.

I stab the stick down, trying to pin its head, and it lunges at the stick. I stomp my boot down right on it, but it dodges and lunges at my leg, gets a mouthful of jeans, and I get my other foot on its body straight away. I gotta keep it from moving, but it's twisting under my boot. It's twisting around to bite at my boot stomped down on its back. I knock its head away with the stick and stab the knife right through it, into the ground, then fall, off balance from shoving both feet and both hands in the same direction fast as I could. I land on my knees, watching the snake with the knife sticking from its head as it twitches and dies.

Snake for the dogs! I laugh, panicky tears running down my face. My hands are still shaking as I cut the snake into seven pieces. One for me and one for Emery too. I give each dog a piece and unclip them from the gang rope, 'cept for Wolf who I drag to sit on the sleeping bag beside Emery. I give them both a piece of snake. Emery looks at it and back at me, then he tears at the skin with his teeth, and chews at the meat just like the dogs are doing.

'We gotta learn to walk on our heads,' he says and laughs, like he don't think it's funny at all to be chewing on raw snake.

'Or turn into a doggo,' I say, sitting down beside him.

'Woof!' he says, and tears at the skin again.

I think we've both gone a bit wild.

EMERY COUNTRY

The snake skin is tough and warm, and the meat is disgusting, but my stomach is so empty it's turning inside out with aching, and it's telling me to put anything into it. So I try not to breathe in the smell, just tear little pieces of meat off the bones and chew and chew till it's not anything but mush, and swallow.

The other dogs are finished, and they come edging around to see if I've got any scraps for them. I keep all the bits of skin and bone I can't eat till the end, and share them out. Then all the dogs drink from the dam, getting mud up their legs, until they're all black on the lower half, and stretch out under the tree next to us and sleep.

We wade into the mud and drink too, chew on some bulrushes till our jaws are sore, then I sleep. Knife one side of me, rifle the other, and five big dogs. The wind flaps the tree branches around above us, but even that don't keep me awake. I'm so tired.

I wake early with the first bit of light and climb to the top of the bank with Roochy and look around. The wind is still wild, parting Maroochy's fur and blowing dust in my eyes, but dust is still the only thing moving out here.

I get the cart and the dogs ready to go again. I check their paws, and poor Squid has a split on his back paw that he's been licking at but he's not limping. I get out the knife and cut him a little boot from the front of my T-shirt and tape it together with a strip of enormous silver tape that I borrow from Emery's arm.

Emery has dark circles under his eyes and his lips are cracked, but he gets another drink and climbs back on the cart. With the morning sun low and in our eyes, we set off again.

We go all morning. Just an hour and a rest and another hour and a rest. We sleep for a while in the middle of the day, in the shade of a big old tree, then we go on again, and I can't hardly even keep watch. I can't even get excited seeing there's clumps of brown grass out here, pushing up through the flat weeds, struggling in the shadow of prickles, grass heads flicking against the cart coz I can't steer round them. My head is so heavy, my arms hard to lift, my legs ache to sit down. My throat is all scratchy dust. The dogs are trotting, heads down. All of us weighed down by dirt and dust and empty bellies. All of us thirsty and so dry we could blow away. But suddenly Maroochy swerves and growls and stops. I haul on the brake. There's a man standing there, beside a pile of scrubby trees, with a rifle pointing right at us.

'Where d'ya think you're going?' he yells.

Emery is on his feet in a flash. Still the big brother. 'We're just passing through!' he yells. 'We don't want no trouble.'

'Where are you heading?' the man asks.

'My ma's place,' Emery says.

'Who's that?' the man asks.

'None of your business,' Emery says.

The man laughs. 'Cheek like that I'd recognise anywhere. You Chrissy's boy?'

Emery nods. 'You know my ma? Is she okay?'

'I seen her two days ago,' he says. 'She trades mushrooms and pumpkins for meat every now and then.' He holds up his other hand and he's got four possums hanging in a bunch by their tails. 'We gotta eat what the land gives us.'

'How far away are we now?' Emery asks.

'Maybe three hours walking,' the man says, and he tilts his head and looks at the dogs. 'Probably two for you if these bags of bones can keep going.' The man unhooks two possums and holds them out to us.

I jump off and run and get them.

'Thank you,' I say.

'You boys look like you been in the wars,' he says.

I look down, the mud, the dust, the torn clothes, the snake blood, and I nod. 'There's mean people back there.'

The man nods too. 'You should push on, see how far you get. You could almost get to the house tonight before it gets too dark. I'll let the others know it's okay to let you through.' He takes out a mirror and flashes it at a distant hill. The hill flashes back.

I hang the possums over the handlebars and open my mouth to tell the man that Mum and Dad are right behind us, but then I look at Emery and he's shaking his head.

'Tell Chrissy it was Mike what loaned you the possums,' the man says. 'She can pay me back.' He winks.

I smile. We've found people who are still nice like us.

197

'Thank you,' I say again and shout, 'Hike! Mush!' to the dogs, and we set off. I wave to Mike.

'We can't go to the house,' Emery says quietly. 'It might be a trap.'

'What?' I say, coz I'm feeling like we're in good country now. We're in a place where people got enough to eat and know Emery's family.

'More meat on a dog than a possum,' Emery says.

'No!' I say. But I know he's right. I know we can't trust no one. I'm just too tired to go on without help.

'I know a place we can hide, near Ma's,' he says. 'If we can get there.'

Lights flash around the valley and now I'm scared they're people organising an ambush, not telling them we're okay to pass. I'm so terrified now, tears leak down my face, no matter that there's no water in me to waste, but I head the cart where Emery tells me, and a while later, when it's almost dark, Emery walks Maroochy and the cart down into a ditch beside an old road, to a pile of enormous concrete tubes and a little trickle of a creek.

'They dumped these here years ago, to do some drainage under the road or something,' Emery says. 'But they never did it.'

I unhook the dogs and shove the cart into a concrete

tube. Crouched in the opening of the tube, I cut up the two possums and feed the dogs right away.

Then we lay out the sleeping bag on the cold hard concrete and crawl onto it. One by one, the dogs slink over looking for a warm bit of sleeping bag for themselves, and I snuggle against a furry back to keep myself warm without my hoodie.

A car rumbles by slowly on the road above us, gravel crunching, lights bouncing around the countryside outside the concrete tube, and the dogs growl, them not having heard a car on a road for so long.

LYING IN THE GROUND

At first light, Maroochy wakes me, nudging my face with her damp nose, and Emery is gone from the sleeping bag beside me. I crawl out of the giant concrete pipe, and there he is, standing, staring around, looking like he knows where he is, holding his arm to his body. He looks like the sleep did him some good. Or maybe he's just excited he's home.

'Come on then,' he says, 'let's get to those caves before the sun comes up. Even if Ma's not there, at least I know my way around, and no one will catch us.'

'They gotta be okay,' I say. 'We've come all this way.'

Emery shakes his head. 'Working real hard for

something doesn't always make it turn out, Bells. Sometimes things just go wrong.'

'I know that,' I say. 'Didn't you see me knowing that back there, when I was driving the dogs on and on, and shooting at a man, and feeding you a hunk of dead snake?'

'Yeah,' Emery says. He reaches over and rubs my head, like Dad always does. 'You're walking on your head real good.'

I smile and pack up the cart quick, even though Emery's standing there saying we'd travel faster just running, but the bumping of the cart is nothing as bad as the bumping of running for his arm and head, plus there's no way either of us can run as fast as a dog, even a dog towing us on a cart.

We're off, the sky behind us grey with new light, like smoky glass, getting lighter all the time, chasing us into the darkness that has kept us hidden most of the journey here.

There are even more tufts of wild grass here, brown and yellow like they're supposed to be, but alive on this old country like they've been for a million years, I bet. Alive after the fungus, they're pushing up through the sprawling weeds.

A small mob of roos bound over a hill ahead of us

and the dogs race on with Emery calling, 'Haw! Rooch! Haw!' to keep Maroochy's starving brain and stomach from chasing them down.

'There's time enough for roo hunting when we're all safe,' Emery says.

I guess the possum last night has helped, coz the dogs mind Emery and we run on.

We dip down between two hills and cross a dry creek bed. All the trees are blackened off here, like a fire came through. Me and Emery hop off and walk. I lift the cart over the lumps of stones, then Emery rides the cart up the hill, while I run along beside, hanging onto the handlebar to steer, coz the dogs are exhausted.

At the top of the hill, I climb back on, and I'm so tired from running up the hill I can hardly lift my knees high enough to get on the step.

Eating a big roast roo sounds like a great idea right now, and I wonder if we can go back for one.

The light catches up to us, so now we can see for ages, and the yellow grass stretches forever from here, like the fungus never made it this far. 'Murphy's farm is down there,' Emery says, pointing. 'They ran goats for meat. Those things went everywhere. I helped them round up a couple of summers ago.' He stares at the tin sheds and long brick house when we get closer. 'I don't think anyone's there.' The sheds and all the fences are blackened.

He looks away and tells Rooch to 'Haw a bit, haw a bit,' to turn us away from those empty Murphy farm buildings. I keep working the brakes as the land dips and lifts, and when we're on top of a small rise, Emery says, 'Woah!' and stops the dogs. He stares down at a square, dirty white house with a couple of big sheds next to it. It's ringed by old cars and bits of rusty tin like a huge wall around it and the road leading to it is just two dirt tracks.

Emery breathes in and lets it go slowly, and he just stares like he doesn't know what the next move is.

'Is that your grandparents' house?' I ask.

He nods. 'Ma said there was nothing here for me, but I would've been happy working in the caves and growing the mushrooms. That big old white van?' He points to a tall van, red dirt halfway up its side, in with the cars that make up the wall around the house. 'Ma used to drive the mushrooms to town in that.'

In the front lawn, there's a mound and a hunk of tin rammed in one end and writing on the tin. It looks like a grave. I'm not close enough to see the writing. It don't look like a word long enough to be 'Christmas'. Emery's and his face is stone cold shocked. All the life gone from his cheeks. He's seen it too. Nothing I can say will calm him down about seeing that. To me, it looks like he don't even want to believe he's seen it. Tears are filling his eyes though, and we gotta keep moving.

I look all around us, coz up here we stand out. 'Do you think they're in there?'

'I dunno. We should go on to the caves.' He jumps back on the cart and turns the dogs again away from the house, shouts 'Mush!' and 'Haw!', like he's afraid of that old house now and who's lying in the ground down there.

EMERY BEACH

We race down through tufty brown grass and scrubby little trees, winding between them up onto a flat, and in the distance, above thousands of scrubby bushes, dark green like a lumpy carpet, there's a bizarre pink bank like the land below it just fell down a bit.

'Are the caves there? In that bank?' I ask.

Emery shakes his head. 'They're here, underneath us. Water cut caves through this bit of land, leaving it so dry on top it looks worthless, but underneath, it's damp enough for growing mushrooms. Ba...' He stops. He swallows. He don't need to tell me he thinks it's his grandad lying in the ground down there on the front lawn. 'Ba bought the house when he was young and foolish, Grandma said, when he found out there was a secret gold mine on the property. He never did find any gold, and water kept seeping in wherever he dug, so Grandma brought logs in and started growing shiitake mushrooms in the mine shafts, and her and Ma picked them and sold them in Swan Hill. Ma said to tell people we were growing them in the sheds, coz the tunnels are probably illegal. You can't see the old mine until you're almost falling into it.'

'Don't let us fall into it,' I say.

Emery guides us around the scrubby trees, shouting, 'Haw!' and 'Gee!' at the dogs, who are just trotting now, and 'Left!' and 'Right!' at me, before he finally grabs one of the handlebars and shoves it around himself.

Anger is working its way through him. I don't know what's going on in his head but it's real bad thoughts about his grandad being dead, I'm guessing.

We wind our way deeper into the scrub and finally it opens out into a clearing with a little concrete creek. The concrete is full of stones, worn and polished shiny sitting set in the concrete, dark where water laps at them.

'This is some old mining thing,' Emery says and waves at it. 'Woah!' he says and stops the dogs. 'We'll shove the cart in there, under the scrub, and get the dogs some water.' Emery points at a bare patch under a gnarly old scrubby tree, so I unhook the dogs one by one from the gang rope and let them go get a drink from the concrete creek. I drink too. So glad to wash the dust from my throat.

I'm afraid to speak in case I say something that'll set Emery off. His body is stiff like he's about to lose it. And why not? He's waited to come back here for so long and when he finally does, his grandad might be dead.

Emery gets down on his belly and drinks too. He looks up at me, the morning light making his dark irises paler and glassy. 'This is the place we come to find, Bell.'

I nod but I don't smile, coz what good is finding a place if the people you love aren't here no more.

I pick up the rifle. 'Where's the mine?' I ask, but Emery don't answer. He splashes over the concrete creek and up into a worn path on the other side. There's an old shed there, with a built-in bench and table, all of it painted patchy green and brown.

'This shed used to be white,' Emery said. 'We kept our buckets here. We'd pick the mushrooms and load them all out to the table, in white buckets.'

'That's a good sign, right?' I ask. 'That they had time

to make sure this was painted and hidden?'

He leads me around the side and down a few steps, the edges lined with planks, to a mine shaft, hidden behind a wall of cut-down scrubby trees, piled up against a hole in the ground. Emery pulls away just one hunk of tree and steps down into the shaft.

It's like a massive rabbit hole going gradual, not straight down, but square. Giant hunks of wood like railway sleepers line the top of the door and down the sides and all along the tunnel leading in. The dogs are dawdling behind us, sniffing and trying to check things out. I pull the lighter out of my pocket and hand it to Emery in case he needs it.

'Twelve steps down,' he says quietly, 'then it levels out. I'll go first and see if anyone's down here.' He holds out his hand and wiggles his fingers for me to hand him the rifle.

I shake my head and hand him the knife. 'You can't shoot with one arm. I'm coming too.' I don't tell him I can't even shoot with two arms.

Emery rolls his eyes. 'Don't trip and shoot me in the back,' he says.

'Don't worry,' I say. 'I only got a couple of bullets. I won't waste them on you.'

He sticks out his tongue. Then he touches his finger to his lips and steps down into the shaft. I follow him, and Maroochy is coming down so close behind me, her head is bumping into my butt. The air is cool and musty down here.

In the dark, Emery gets ahead of me. I don't know how far ahead till he flicks the lighter and lights up a long cave.

'Nobody here,' he says. But I'm not looking at him. The walls are lined with racks of weird logs and growing out of those strange stringy logs are hundreds of glorious white mushrooms, long bent stalks with delicate wavy caps. The way they stick out from the wall with their little circle caps all parallel and perfectly white makes me think of a pile of hovering alien space ships. Are these even Earthling food? I pull the cap off one and shove it in my mouth. It's dry and squeaky on my teeth, but it's food.

'These are shiitake,' Emery says. 'They're looking real healthy, so someone's taking care of them.'

Rooch sniffs at the mushrooms, so does Bear, and the other dogs are coming down behind her. She sniffs at me eating one, like she's not sure. I pluck another cap off a log and break it up and give it to her. She's hungry enough to eat anything, but she's chewing it with her mouth open, lips back, like it's not a taste she likes.

I grab some more and break them up and pop them in front of Bear and Oyster and Squid, and even Wolf, slinking in the shadows, not wanting to be left alone.

'Come on, Wolf,' I say and crumble a mushroom for him. 'It's just until we go get you a nice fat roo.'

Squid gets a real taste for them and bites a few mushrooms off the racks on the wall. Chewing and pushing them out again with his tongue and picking them up off the damp cave floor for another go, like he's not sure he wants them in his mouth or out. He's such a goose.

Emery yelps and takes his thumb off the hot lighter.

'What now?' I ask him in the dark.

'Grab the sleeping bag. We'll go on into the other tunnels and wait to see who comes down. Most mushrooms don't need extra water, but these mushrooms are from damp mountain forests in Asia, and they need a bit of a spray to keep them growing.'

I run out and get the sleeping bag from the cart and head back down. Emery leads us further into the tunnels and along a little channel of water, and finally there's a light ahead. It's a crack of light in the rock.

'This tunnel was made by water seeping into a

crack and washing it out over the years,' he says. Emery squeezes through the crack, the rocks on either side worn smooth like lots of people been squeezing through here. I follow him through, pushing back Roochy's head, coz she thinks we can both fit at the same time, her not wanting to wait till I've dragged the sleeping bag through.

The cave, which is all pale pink and white rock, is lit up good from that jagged crack above, and it opens out wide enough so I can walk with my arms out and drag my fingers either side, and then it widens further, just in one bit and the floor is all pale sand with a hollowed-out side of the wall, almost the shape of our tent.

'And this is Emery Beach,' Emery says, and he smiles soft like he's remembering good times.

'So you got your own beach?' I say. 'How come you never told me about this place?'

Emery shrugs with one shoulder. 'It's a secret place.'

It's real weird to have a beach way down under the ground with just a jagged crack of light above, coz it's not warm or sunny like a regular beach. It's cold.

'Well, it's not so secret with that shaft of light lighting up the end of the mine tunnel,' I say.

'Yeah,' Emery agrees. 'It was pretend secret for when I was a kid, same age as you.'

'Ha!' I laugh. There's been no time for me pretending like a kid in the last two weeks.

So we take turns at sitting in the dark of the mushroom mine tunnel with the rifle or sleeping curled up in a sleeping bag on the tent surrounded by dogs, me winding my fingers into Roochy's fur to feel safe.

Nobody comes down to water the mushrooms, but I play over saying, 'Hello, Christmas? Is that you?' in my head a million times.

A BLACK KANGAROO?

When the light in the crack above Emery Beach loses its glare, Emery says we need to go get some possums or roos for the dogs, and this idea is full of problems. Emery can't run, I can't cut the throat of an animal even to stop it suffering, I can't even think of it, not unless it's a snake that looks like it might bite me or the dogs.

If the dogs get wind of something and take off, they'll be howling up the place letting anyone around know there's a pack of dogs in the scrub and they might come looking.

'The dogs just gotta eat mushrooms tonight,' I say. 'Until we find out who is around. Hunting is too noisy.

You keep them quiet in here and I'll go back and check out the house.'

'Ella, no!' Emery says. 'I know my way around. I should go.'

I shake my head and hand him the rifle. 'You can't run.'

'There's other tunnels Ma could be hiding in. She might not even be in the house,' Emery says. And it's like he's been thinking the worst while we've been waiting all day down here.

'If I don't see anyone in the house, then we'll check those out, tomorrow,' I say.

'Ella, I need to come with you!' he says, and he winds his fingers around my arm so hard it hurts.

He really needs to know who is dead down there. And who is alive.

'I know,' I say. 'You need to know. But I need you to keep the dogs quiet. I can do this. I'll just look and come straight back.'

'Take Rooch then. She'll keep you safe.'

I nod, coz I'm worried about getting lost in the dark and Rooch will help me find my way back through all that scrub to Emery.

So it's me and Rooch alone again. Me walking with

my hand tight around Maroochy's collar, us picking our way down between the trees towards the house.

We sneak up on it until the last scrubby bush before the house. Mike, the guy who gave us the possums, is striding down the road, a rifle slung over one shoulder, a small roo and a few possums over the other. He gets to the old van and he slaps on the door.

'Chrissy!' he yells and my heart leaps. She's in there, everything is okay!

'Hold on!' Christmas yells from the house, and then she comes down the steps, the sight of her sending my heart pounding and my eyes to tears. Then she disappears behind the tin and old car fence. The scrape of a sliding van door, and then she's inside the van with the window in the other door beside Mike slid open.

'Those boys turn up?' Mike asks, his voice carries across the early evening air. Roochy growls softly.

'What boys?'

'Your boy and another one,' Mike says. 'And a pack of dogs.'

'Emery?' Christmas asks, and her voice is so full of hope, I almost leap up then and there and yell, 'It's us, we're here! We're okay!' But Rooch is growling about Mike, and Rooch knows things.

215

'I'd know him anywhere. He was on his way here, should've been here by now. I gave them two possums, so you owe me.'

Christmas is looking out across the land like she's looking for Emery. I duck down lower into the scrubby grass. 'He hasn't got here yet,' she says.

'I didn't pass him, so the kid must be hiding out somewhere. Still I gave him two possums, you owe me.'

'Of course, if you helped Emery, I'm happy to give you mushrooms,' Christmas says.

'What do you mean, "if"?' Mike growls.

'I mean, I'm sure you did,' Chrissy says, her voice careful and calm like Mike might be dangerous. 'I've got half a bucket picked already, but the rest can't be picked too early, they're gonna need another couple of days growing. I can give you another half bucket in two days. And a pumpkin.'

Mike nods. 'Thanks. Do you want to trade for the roo as well?'

Maroochy whines and pulls at my hand like she wants to get moving. I pull her back down.

'I'm all out of mushrooms,' Christmas says, like she hasn't got a whole cave full. 'You wait here, and I'll go get you that half bucket from the shed.'

216

Christmas climbs out of the van and slides the door shut hard behind her. Then she hurries out behind the house checking the hillsides all around her, like she's looking for Emery maybe. Or Mike's men. There's a flash up high somewhere in the hills off to the side. Mike hasn't seen it.

'Don't you let that bloody horse trader rip you off!' an old lady yells from the house. Emery's grandma is down there too.

Chrissy's back from the sheds soon enough carrying a white bucket.

Maroochy whines and pulls away from me. I lunge after her, but I fall and get a faceful of dry grass as she streaks away. I get up and chase after her. Too scared to call for her in case Mike turns.

The two of us charging flat out towards the house, and I think that somehow Rooch knows that something is going to happen or that she knows that Christmas is Emery's mum, coz she lets out these happy yips like she does when she's saying hello to one of us, but she swings away from the house.

Mike turns around at the sound of the yips and he puts down his roo and possums. I swerve from following Maroochy and run flat out towards Mike and he's so far

217

away and he starts doing what I hope he won't do. He's pulling his gun off his shoulder. What does he think she is? A black kangaroo?

THE FLASHING HILLS

My legs are hardly keeping up with my body as Mike's hand, fingers holding something shiny, goes from his pocket to his rifle, and back to his pocket a second time and I'm running, not breathing, no air in me, no air to even scream. He lifts his rifle and points it right at Maroochy, and I open my mouth but nothing comes out, and the rifle lifts higher and it's not pointing at Maroochy. It's pointing up to the road. And there's flashing. Mirrors flashing the last of the light all around in the hills, and something is happening but I don't know what.

And coming down the road, slowly, on a silent white bike is two people. A tall woman and a thin small man with his head close shaven like mine. Mum and Dad! My throat lets out an enormous sob.

Mike lines up the rifle and his finger slides forwards to the trigger, and all the time I'm running, running, can't run any faster. I yell and leap, pull my fists into my body and twist my shoulder forwards and hit him full on in the side, my shoulder hurting as it connects with his ribs and he falls against the van with a thump. The rifle drops to the ground, and I scramble over him, his hands snatching at my shirt. I grab the rifle and keep running. Mum and Dad have seen Maroochy, yipping and sprinting across the flat. They're off their bike. Standing up, putting the bike stand down. Standing still.

Dad always said hardly anybody in Australia can shoot straight, so if you're a long way off, keep running. And now there he is, standing still, him not knowing there's guns all around him and Mum.

'The hills!' I yell, but maybe they haven't even seen me. And maybe they can't hear me over Rooch's yipping.

Then 'Crack!' a shot rings out from somewhere up on the hill.

Stones fly up on the road in front of Mum and Dad, pinging off the plastic and metal of the bike. They scramble and duck down behind the bike.

Me and Maroochy, we're still running though. Maroochy lower to the ground. Nothing is gonna stop her from getting to Dad after all this time.

I slide to a stop. Drop down sitting on one leg, with one knee out in front of me. I stick the butt of the rifle in my hip and rest it on my knee and hold it down with all the strength I have in one hand. Line up my knee to where I think the shot came from up the hill. I have no hope of really aiming a rifle. I pull the trigger.

The gun slams into my hip. The crack makes my ears go numb, my fingers buzz and burn.

'Wait!' Mike yells. He's running after me.

Behind him, Christmas is climbing out of the van, screaming, 'You leave them kids alone!'

I get up and run, all of us running flat out towards Mum and Dad, still ducked down behind the bike.

'You tell them guys to stop shooting!' Christmas screams.

Mike's waving his arms as he runs, maybe so they don't shoot him.

Roochy's reached the bike. She's scrabbling around it to leap on Mum and Dad like she's not seen them for a million years. Me too, Roochy. Me too!

'It's okay!' Mike's yelling. He's standing in the middle

of the flat, hands on his knees, puffing. He lifts a hand up to the hills.

I'm gasping when I reach the bikes. I lay the gun down and throw myself into the mess of dog and people that I love, gasping laughing and gasping crying, coz I never thought I'd see them again.

Mum's shouting, 'Ella, baby, are you okay? Where's Emery?'

And all I can do is nod and laugh and bawl.

And Dad wraps me in a hug so tight and strong that I want to live there forever. Forever safe in those skinny wiry arms. That man built of wire and steel poles that no one can kill.

Mike arrives and picks up his gun from where I dropped it, and Dad scrambles up. Mum pulls out a revolver and points it at him.

Christmas arrives, slapping at Mike's arm, while he's still holding his gun.

'Them's family, Mike,' she says, telling him off. 'That's my boy's dad and his wife.' Then she's around the back of the bike hugging Mum, never minding about the revolver, and then hugging Dad and scooping me up and hugging me too. 'Where's my boy?' she's whispering in my ear, like she's gotta know right now.

And I know I gotta keep the secret of the mushroom caves from Mike, so I say, 'Just in the scrub there. He's got a broken arm but he's sitting there happy as anything on a bit of sand he's calling Emery Beach.'

Christmas plants a big kiss on my cheek and says, 'I'll go get him.'

'Need a hand, Chrissy?' Mike offers.

'No,' Chrissy says, waving Mike's offer away with her hand. 'The boy's dad will help me. He'll be wanting to see him.'

Dad grins. 'I am.'

'You go get your mushrooms by the van, Mike,' Christmas says, all bossy. 'And I'll have that other half bucket and a pumpkin for you in two days' time like I promised, but after that, I don't think we'll be able to spare any. Not with the whole family home now.'

And I'm so happy with the sound of that. The whole family home now. We really are. The whole family. Home together.

'But Chrissy,' Mike says, 'we agreed we all got to contribute to the community.'

'Well, with more help, maybe I can get more mushrooms and veggies turned out next month, but I'm taking it down to the village to trade. I'm sick of your manky soup possums. Sometimes I think you been taking advantage of me since my dad died and I been stuck home looking after my mum.'

I suck in a breath. 'Ba's dead? Emery's gonna be so upset.'

Christmas nods and rubs my cheek. Her touch so soft. She blinks a couple of times, and says so gently, like she's breaking bad news to just me alone, 'Was only medicine keeping him going and we couldn't get it sent in here anymore. That's just how it was. We all knew it would come to that. Especially after he set the land on fire to burn off that bad grass. Nearly killed himself doing that burn-off.'

'He went mad,' Mike says. 'Nearly burned down everybody's properties!'

'Well that mad old man and his burn-off and his seeds is the only reason you're still eating possum and roo today, Mike, so you owe him,' Christmas says. 'A few lost houses for all that grass coming back was a fair trade. Off you go! Make sure your trigger-happy men don't shoot you.'

Mike twists his lips to one side but sets off back across the flat to the van left wide open.

'He's a bit right,' Christmas says. 'My father was

working on the old idea of burning off grasslands like they used to do when there was just Australian grasses. But those damn dormant English grasses, all dried up and black and sick, made the fire burn too hot. Got out of control. Killed off the roots he was hoping to save, burnt down a few houses. Poor man went 'round trying to reseed the whole county after that. Exhausted himself and never got better.' Chrissy takes a deep breath. 'Mike's been making my life a misery ever since. I'm so glad you're here now.' Christmas looks at Mum. 'Can you ride down there ahead of him, make sure he doesn't get in through the van. I don't want him poking around in the sheds.'

Mum hops back on the bike, and says, 'Come on, then,' to me, so I climb on the back and we head off after Mike, passing him as he's halfway, and get to the van before him. Maroochy chases us, yipping at our wheels, then gallops off back to Dad.

Mum parks the bike right in front of the van's sliding door and sits on the van step while I pick up the bucket of mushrooms for Mike and hand it to him when he arrives. He gathers up his roo and possums, and trudges off back towards the road.

I sit on the step beside Mum. She pulls me close and

runs her hand over my stubbly hair. 'Was that my baby bowling a man over, stealing his gun and coming to our rescue?' she asks.

'Not a baby no more,' I say.

'You did it, Els. You got Emery and the dogs here. I'm so proud of you.'

I poke Mum in the side. 'And I'm real proud of you for finding Dad. Never leave me again!'

Mum laughs.

WAGGLING WINGS

Life's good at Christmas's with us all there together. Chrissy has pumpkins winding their way all over her back yard, as well as having kept piles of powdered milk from two years before. She says she'll only admit to milk if someone nearby has a baby they can't feed. In the meantime, we're boiling up our mushrooms in milk and they taste amazing.

She hoots and laughs and holds her cheeks when Emery tells her what's in the anthills.

'My father told me to send Emery to the anthills!' She calls him 'my father' now instead of Ba so she doesn't disturb his rest. 'I thought he was going mad!' she says.

'I kept saying, but Emery's not here, and he just kept saying Emery will be here soon, like he knew you were on your way.'

Emery leads us all up to the closest anthill and we crack it open. Beautiful, tiny, round grains tumble out, so shiny in the sunlight they look like mini pearls. Glossy with a hint of green.

I drop to my knees and run my fingers through them. The grains purr as they bump against each other, and the smell, the fresh smell, as each perfect shiny grain slides through my fingers, this is amazing.

'I know he planted a lot of this stuff, but I didn't know he'd stored so much!' Christmas says.

We grind up a little of the grain and make some bread to celebrate us all being together. It's damp and nutty on the inside and crisp and crunchy on the outside, and even though it's so delicious, we pack the rest of in plastic bags and Christmas takes the grains to town and hands them out to people who used to grow wheat or canola. She tells them to plant them across their land so the kangaroos have more to eat, and get fat and healthy, and says, maybe one day we'll have enough to start the bakery back up. She tells them that if the fungus comes back, just burn the grasses same as her dad did and wait for them to grow again. This time the fires won't get out of control, because there's no English grasses lying round browned off or sleeping through the summer adding too much heat.

Emery's arm sets pretty good after a couple of weeks resting in the house in the front window, 'on watch' with his grandma, eating lots of pumpkin soup. I dunno, but I think that time just sitting with his grandma, watching out over his grandad's grave and talking about old times, I think that has healed his heart somehow, along with his arm and that deep gash in his scalp. Winter sets in hard, the pumpkins die off, and we black out the windows and sleep in the lounge room, huddled round the fire. The nights stay cool, even when the hot days come back. We run low on mushrooms coz we have to give so many more away. Dad and Emery are compressing old wood into logs, and Christmas and Grandma work all day in the lab in the shed, seeding the logs, getting them ready for me and Mum to take to the tunnels. The tunnels don't change their temperature much, no matter how cool or hot it is up top, so we can grow lots more mushrooms, but everyone else in town can only grow their vegetables under plastic coz of the cold, so now we're giving mushrooms away or taking IOUs. Our stored pumpkins run out too, so our meals get smaller for a while.

Now Emery's off with Dad every day, hunting for meat to keep the dogs fed. He always carries a bag of seed and he spreads it wherever he goes. He says his grandfather was right. He'd always be here waiting for Emery when he came back. He's in the land, he's in the grasses that he's saved, he's in the knowledge that he's passed to Emery like his people have been doing for thousands of generations, he's here as sure as if he was still alive.

Dad keeps watch from the hills some days with Mike's men, but there's not many people who come heading up these old roads, them probably thinking it's too dry out here to grow anything. Those that do look like they've been driven out of every other place, blank eyes sunk into bony skulls, so Mike's men tell them they can stay in the old hotel in town, and there's possum and roo and a few veggies if they work, but not much else to eat. Dad says the people mostly look grateful just for that.

'Must be bad out there,' Chrissy says, 'if going into debt to Mike for his manky soup possums looks like a good idea.'

Some days Dad and Emery come back without meat and it's just the eels that me and Christmas pull from the dam for the dogs. Christmas knows how to cook eel and make it tasty enough for us to eat too.

We're down there one night, setting the hooks with chunks of possum tail, when Mum comes down to tell us to look up at the glorious sunset.

It is glorious, orange and gold, and it's like a mash-up of my whole world, the pink dirt, the dry yellow grasses that Emery's grandad planted, the dark trees, patchy red and pink hillsides, even the old dirty white house is every tone of red and yellow there ever was at once.

In the sky, a long way off, there's two little planes flying up and down and back and forth making patterns in the sky. As they get closer, Mum gasps.

'They're dropping something!'

I look back to the house, and I think we can get there before the planes arrive, but Mum takes off towards them.

'Mum!' I yell.

Christmas grabs my hand and we run after her.

The plane sees us and turns towards us, flying low, giving its wings a waggle, and something rains down from the plane as it passes over the top of us. I cover my face, thinking it must be poison or something, but tiny things ping off my head and neck.

Mum turns back and runs at me with her arms up. Her eyes are wide. 'Grass!' she screams. 'They're grass seeds!'

She scoops me up and spins me around, then hugs

Christmas and they leap up and down together, screaming, 'Grass! Grass! Grass!'

On the side of the grey airforce plane I see the words 'CSIRO Seed Bank'. And I didn't even know this was a thing. That someone was working hard to find enough seeds to spread everywhere. Enough to spread over the Mallee grasslands, and maybe the Wimmera grasslands to the south too. Maybe the whole country? Or just the big grasslands? Maybe the wheat fields are already planted with wheat? I wish I knew. I hope the starving people in the cities know that spring grass is coming, and they only have to hold out awhile longer.

I drop to my knees and scoop together some of the grains, and in amongst the spiky grains, the fluffy grains, the short grains, the fat grains, the long pale grains, the green and the yellow grains, I'm sure there's the same round grain that came spilling out of Emery's anthills.

Emery's tearing down the hill at us coz he's heard us screaming, five dogs and Dad on his heels, and he laughs like a clown when he figures out why we're so happy.

I show Emery the grains I've caught, all the different shapes and sizes and some just like his grandad's.

Emery nods. 'He said the old grass doesn't care if the overseas grass grows first and dies down, it makes the

232

soil healthy and covers the ground, which the old grass likes, and each grass will grow where it grows best no matter what farmers plant. He said people are like grass seeds, you can dig them in and feed them someplace, and maybe they'll grow quickly there for a while but only the ones that really suit that place will thrive.'

'That's why he said you could come back after high school?' I ask. 'Coz you needed to find out where you'd thrive?'

Emery smiles. 'I guess. I never thought of that.'

'They must have figured out how to control the fungus,' Dad says, turning the seeds over in his hand, right under his nose, like the answer is written on the sides of the seeds and he just needs glasses to read it. 'Or maybe how to make the grass resistant?'

Christmas starts making plans. 'After grass, there'll be grain and bread, so I'm gonna have me the biggest sandwich, with a fine slice of salami and huge chunk of cheese, coz there'll be cows, and an egg, coz there'll be chooks, runny in the middle, firm around the outside. Then for dessert, mmm, ice-cream!'

Emery runs and grabs his mum, and says, 'I'm gonna have me a doughnut. Crispy, right outta the fryer, hot jam in the middle and a blob of cream on top, all melting.'

'What'll you have, Ella?' Dad asks.

'Anzac bickies,' I say, even if I can't remember what they taste like no more. 'A family-sized tin and I'll eat them all myself until they ooze out my eyeballs!'

'You know none of this stuff will be here this year, right? Maybe not for years,' Dad asks.

I smile. 'But it's coming.'

'And when it does,' Dad says, 'I think everyone is going to be a little more careful.'

Him and Mum have been talking about staying up here for good, helping Christmas with her business, getting solar set up on the house, helping out the rest of the town with solar or crank electricity coz solar panels are hard to find, farming roos and eels to sell meat to nearby towns. There's lots to do here and I'm happy coz I like it here, where the dogs get to run all day and there's always someone around and we can all look out for each other.

The plane comes back around waggling its wings and the pilot is grinning and waving, his face orange in the sunset.

I leap about, waving back at him, chasing after him, five big doggos leaping and yowling, chasing him too. Me, waving and waving, wild and happy coz I thought

234

everyone had given up, just decided to look out for themselves, but someone, somewhere, made a seed bank to save the seeds just like Emery's grandad did, and they're finally replanting grass, even way out here.

ACKNOWLEDGEMENTS

I hope that *The Dog Runner* will get young people thinking and talking about the ways we currently manage our environment, where we source our food, and what we eat. Food security is an important issue, easily overlooked, and Australia is an interesting place to consider this, as it was extensively and successfully managed and farmed prior to the arrival of Europeans, their animals and plants.

I would like to acknowledge the traditional owners of the lands on which this book is set and pay my respects to their Elders past and present. In addition, I would like to convey my respect of their past care and management of these lands and waterways, and highlight to others that this custodial work and the accumulation and passing down of landcare knowledge has never ceased and is ongoing around the country by many groups, including these groups in Victoria:

Barengi Gadjin Land Council, Horsham
Eastern Maar Aboriginal Corporation, Melbourne
Bunurong Land Council Aboriginal Corporation, Frankston

Dja Dja Wurrung Clans Aboriginal Corporation, Bendigo

Taungurung Clans Aboriginal Corporation, Broadford

I deeply respect the work done on-country by these groups and others, continuing to manage their land and waterways, sustaining cultural traditions, regenerating native species, protecting cultural sites, and providing job opportunities and training programs for local Indigenous people. I believe their work should be supported as their knowledge of land management and native species is vital to our future.

Thank you so much Jared Thomas for reading The Dog Runner, and for your thoughtful advice and support. Thanks also to John Clarke, Director at Eastern Maar Aboriginal Corporation, for taking the time to comment on the need to build relationships with communities when depicting practices belonging to particular Aboriginal communities.

I read these books as I wrote *The Dog Runner* and highly recommend them:

Dark Emu by Bruce Pascoe

The Biggest Estate on Earth by Bill Gammage

I received a Neilma Sidney Literary Travel Grant from The Myer Foundation and Writers Victoria to assist with research travel for this book, and I thank them for their support in visiting the regions Ella and Emery travelled, walking railway trails, and also meeting with the following people:

Graeme Hand at Stipa in Branxholme, thank you for meeting with me and detailing the process of natural grassland regeneration. Thank you for your fascinating insights and walk of your demonstration farm. It was quite terrifying to learn how out of tune modern farming is with our land. Soil health is everything, a vital fact understood by the original farmers of Australia, but now largely ignored as farmers push the land to its limits to meet the bills.

Emily Vourlidis, President of Sled Dog Racing Queensland, thanks for meeting me at 6am on a cold morning, answering questions, and allowing me to see sled dogs in action. Kids, if you have a big dog with lots of energy who likes to pull you places look into this wonderful sport. Like Ella and Emery you do not need snow!

Noel Arrol, owner of Li-Sun Exotic Mushrooms, Mittagong, thanks for the tour of your mushroom tunnel and sharing your extensive knowledge of woodland fungi, and a punnet of delicious mushrooms.

Also, a big thank you to Susannah Chambers for all your support and calm advice. I promise one day I'll write a book and not have a major catastrophe during the edits. Thanks to Matariki Williams and the team at Allen & Unwin for all the work you did and do to get this book out to the world. Thank you also Jo Hunt for another brilliant cover.

Thanks to my family, friends and fellow writers for their continued support, and to my husband for narrowly escaping death, being still alive is a pretty big achievement considering, and thanks to Darwin Royal Hospital for rebuilding shattered bones. And now... onto the next adventure!

ABOUT THE AUTHOR

Bren MacDibble was raised on farms all over New Zealand, so is an expert about being a kid on the land. After 20 years in Melbourne, Bren recently sold everything, and now lives and works in a bus travelling around Australia. In 2018, *How to Bee* – her first novel for younger readers – won the Australian Book Council Book of the Year Award for Younger Readers, the New South Wales Premier's Literary Award Patricia Wrightson Prize for Children's Literature and the New Zealand Book Awards, Wright Family Foundation Esther Glen Award for Junior Fiction. Bren also writes for young adults under the name Cally Black.

www.macdibble.com

HOW TO BEE

By Bren MacDibble

How the story starts - a taster

PEONY PEST

Today! It's here! Bright and real and waiting. The knowing of it bursts into my head so big and sudden, like the crack of morning sun busting through the gap at the top of the door. I fall out of my bunk and hit the packing-box floor. I scramble up, right into Gramps asleep in his chair in front of the potbelly stove.

'Cha!' he growls.

'Sorry, Gramps,' I say. 'It's bee day.' I pull on my pest vest and try to squeeze past him, but he holds out his foot.

'First eat, then bee,' he says, real firm. He cuts a wedge from the oatcake on top of the stove.

Cockies screech loud from the tree over our shack. They know it's time to get moving. 'I can't,' I say and try to squeeze past again. 'Foreman's waiting.'

My sister, Magnolia, sticks her fluffy head out from the top bunk. 'Stomp yourself, Peony-pest,' she groans.

'You won't diz me when I'm a bee,' I say.

'P the bee? Yeah, dying for that,' Mags says and flops back on the bunk. But she won't diz me when I'm a bee. Everyone likes bees. Urbs come out in buses from the city just to see bees work. The Urbs cling to the bus windows as the buses travel up and down between the rows of blossoms, and if they ever look out the back window after they pass me in my boring green pest vest, they'll see me standing there with my rude finger up, telling them how I feel about them getting all the fruit we work so hard to make.

I grab the oatcake from Gramps, duck around him and push through the sacking-lined door.

My chooks cluck when they see me and I flick the catch on the coop door. They push out and peck at the grass. 'I'm not doing pests today,' I tell them. 'You have to get your own. I'm a bee now.' I crumble some of my oatcake, so they cluck all happy around my feet. 'Mags is still a pest, she'll find you something to eat.' Mags is too big and clumsy to ever be a bee. I take a bite of oatcake and crumble the rest and scatter it so I can get away without chooks on my tail.

Sometimes bees get too big to be up in the branches, sometimes they fall and break their bones. This week both happened and Foreman said, 'Tomorrow we'll find two new bees.'

ME AND AJ

I race to the meeting point down in apples, but eleven
pests are already there. I smile at my friend Applejoy and
he smiles back. It's gonna be him and me, like always.

'Peony? Are you ten yet?' Foreman asks when he sees
me. His fluffy eyebrows push down towards his nose.

'Yeah, Boz,' I lie and look all caz.

He nods, and I join the other kids waiting.

Pomegranate digs me in the back with her pointy
finger to tell me she knows I'm lying.

'Cha,' I whisper.

Foreman tells us what to do to try-out to be a bee.
I've seen bees working. I know how it's done. He hands

us a leather cord, and when we all have one, Foreman says, 'Go!'

The pests rush first to the pile of poles and then to the feather box and scuffle over the feathers. I get my pole and stand back. I don't need those old rummaged-through muck feathers. I reach into my pocket and pull out feathers from my chooks. The best bum fluff. The softest fluffiest feathers. I lash them to the end of my wand just like I seen bees do and then I run to Foreman. 'I done, Boz,' I say.

He checks my lashing, nods and hands me a pouch of stamens. He nods towards the trees. 'Row one.'

I'm proud like I'm gonna bust. This is how I always imagined. Me, first with the lashing.

I run fast down to the apple trees. Pomegranate is right behind me. She got a nod from Foreman and she's running to row two.

I'm light. I'm quick. But Pomz can run along fence tips wide as my thumb. I seen her practising. She's long keen on being a bee.

I scramble into the branches of the first tree. Old, thick and spread wide, easy. I dip my wand into the pouch. The other end tangles in the branches. Pomz dips hers on the ground before she climbs. I'm too stupid for not remembering that's how bees do it. I check over my shoulder. Foreman's busy checking lashings. Maybe he's not seen me do it wrong.

I pull the end of the wand out from the branches and start along a branch. A stick jams in my legs and I trip and fall straight out of the tree. I land on my stomach on the dirt. Pomz sniggers and scrambles up her tree. She's stuck the end of her wand into my legs!

'Cha!' I whisper and scramble to my feet. Foreman don't like bees who fight. He's ripped bee vests right off the backs of bees who fight. I climb back into my tree. Foreman's still busy. Didn't see me fall, but I've lost my lead. Pomz is already doing one side of her tree.

I flick the feathers from flower to flower, every flower I can reach, and coz I'm fast and light and a good climber I can pretty much reach them all. This tree will have lots of fruit soon and Foreman will remember that the first row was the one Peony done.

Pomz is running up the main branches of her tree without hanging onto anything. She's heavier than me but faster coz of her balance. She jumps down and runs to her next tree.

Applejoy has his lashing nodded and he runs past to row four just as I jump from my first tree. 'Go, P!' he says.

'Go, Aaj,' I say back. I dip the wand in my pouch, with a big show in case Foreman's watching, so he can see I did it proper, before I climb the tree. The pouch is already half empty. I don't know if I'll have enough to finish the whole row. I spilled some when I fell. I don't want to tell Foreman I spilled some, so when he comes to check my skills I just smile.

'Good bee,' he says.

I'm full to busting again. I will be a bee today!

Other Fiction titles by Australian authors available from Old Barn Books:

The Stars at Oktober Bend, by Glenda Millard
(shortlisted for the CILIP Carnegie Medal 2017)

Alice Nightingale is fifteen, with hair as red as fire and skin as pale as bone, but something inside her is broken.

Manny James runs at night, trying to escape his memories. He sees Alice on the roof of her river-house, looking like a figurehead on a ship sailing through the stars. He has a poem in his pocket and he knows the words by heart. He is sure that girl has written them.

'Surprising, lyrical and beautiful, this book speaks of hope in the darkest of times, and of love in its many forms. The voices of Alice and Manny are distinctive and memorable, and their resilience will stay with me…' Liz Flanagan, author of Eden Summer

A Small Free Kiss in the Dark, by Glenda Millard

Skip's an outsider, a quiet observer. He draws pictures to make sense of the world. He's never fitted in. So he takes to the streets. Life there may be hard, but it's better than the one he's left behind, especially when he teams up with old Billy. Then come the bombs which leave little Max in his care, and also Tia, the sad dancer, with her sweet baby, Sixpence. Scavenging for food, sheltering in an empty funfair, living on love and imagination… how long can Skip's fragile new family hold out as war grips the city?

A Different Dog, by Paul Jennings

The forest is dense and dark. And the trail full of unexpected perils. The dog can't move. The boy can't talk. And you won't know why. Or where you are going. You will put this story down to not wanting the journey to end. But it's from Paul Jennings so watch out for the ambush.

A Different Boy, by Paul Jennings

The orphanage is far behind. But life as a stowaway is even worse. And nothing is what it seems on this sea of troubles. Will Anton survive? Can you guess the shocking truth? Another compelling tale from the master storyteller. Nominated for the CILIP Carnegie Medal 2019.